California
DEMON

California DEMON

MARILYN SINGER

Hyperion Books for Children
New York

FIRST EDITION

1   3   5   7   9   10   8   6   4   2

Library of Congress Cataloging-in-Publication Data

Singer, Marilyn.
California demon/Marilyn Singer—1st ed.
p. cm.
Summary. When Rosie accidentally releases an imp from a bottle in
her mother's magic shop, he ends up in California, where he causes
great havoc until Rosie convinces her mother to teach her witchcraft
so that she can help recapture him.
ISBN 1-56282-298-5 (trade)—ISBN 1-56282-299-3 (lib. bdg.)
[1. Magic—Fiction. 2. Fairies—Fiction. 3. Witches—Fiction.]
I. Title.
PZ7.S6172Cal   1992
[Fic]—dc20   92-52981   CIP   AC

Grateful acknowledgment is made for permission
to reprint the following copyrighted material: Excerpt from
"I Want To Be Happy"
(Irving Caesar, Vincent Youmans)
© 1924 WB MUSIC CORP., IRVING CAESAR MUSIC CORP. (Renewed)
All Rights Reserved. Used By Permission.

To Don and Leah

Thanks to Steve Aronson, Kathleen Cotter,
Ellen Goldstein, Jay Kerig, Aston McKen, Asher Williams,
and, especially, Liz Gordon and Andrea Cascardi.

California
DEMON

Chapter One

Exactly one week before Christmas, at 1:45 on an afternoon as cold and snowy as only a December afternoon in Vermont can be, Rosie Rivera sat tied to a chair in the basement of her mother's magic shop, listening to the sounds of bumping and crashing on the floor above.

If only, she thought miserably. Are there any crummier words in the English language? If only. If only I were beautiful. If only Johnny Haines liked me. If only I hadn't tried to make a love potion to get Johnny Haines to like me. And, especially, if only I hadn't opened the wrong bottle by mistake and let out that nasty little imp who's upstairs wreaking heaven knows what havoc.

Rosie sighed, then frowned. It's Lydia's fault, really. If only she'd taught me how to make a proper love potion in the first place, everything would have been fine. But

Lydia won't teach me a thing. She doesn't want me to learn magic. Heck, she doesn't even want to practice it herself. Real magic, that is—not those silly games and party tricks she demonstrates and sells upstairs. I mean, honestly, what good is it having a witch for a mother if she doesn't want to be one?

The ceiling rattled above her head. Lydia's going to kill me when she gets back. Rosie sighed again, more mournfully than before. Then the sigh turned to a shudder. If that creature doesn't kill me first, she thought, and she opened her mouth to scream for help, but all that came out was a goose's honk—and a feeble one at that. For her second attempt she mooed like a cow. No wonder the imp hadn't bothered to gag her. It obviously found the idea of Rosie sounding like a barnyard far more amusing.

Rosie pursed her lips. Okay, Rivera, she told herself, one thing Lydia *did* teach you is to look at the bright side of things. Maybe the imp will get bored and go back in its bottle. A bone-jarring thump and the shatter of glass told her this hadn't happened yet. She winced, but bravely persisted. And when it gets bored and goes back in its bottle, a customer will come and find me before Lydia does. Then I'll straighten up the mess and she'll never know what happened.

Bang! Smash! Rosie winced again and had to admit it was hopeless. Face it, girl. That bottle was dated 1928. If you'd been stuck in a bottle over sixty years, would you want to go back inside? Furthermore, there hasn't been a customer all day—which, as if things aren't bad enough, will really drive Lydia crazy, it being nearly Christmas and

2

she's been threatening to close the store if business doesn't pick up—and I can't imagine anyone will come in now, with what's going on up there. *Thud! Splat!*

Oh no, Rosie moaned, and she strained hard against the thin cords the imp had wrapped around her until, exhausted, she fell back in her seat.

Suddenly, all the hideous noise ceased. A moment later, cutting through the silence, came the clear, sweet ring of the door chimes. A customer, Rosie exalted. At last.

Upstairs, the imp was also delighted to see a buyer. With a wave of his hand, he cleaned up the mess he'd made.

"Hello, hello, hello!" he greeted the thin, balding, well-dressed man who'd just entered the shop. "It's a pleasure to serve you. The customer's always right. Do unto others as you'd have them do unto you. Have a nice day." The imp flashed a big toothy grin, then took out his teeth and laid them, still grinning, on the counter.

The man, Adam Pauling by name, frowned. He was in a hurry—as a matter of fact, he was always in a hurry. A traveling salesman, he spent his time whizzing from one town to another. He liked to tell people he'd seen all of New England—and none of it. His customers found this funny. His ex-wife and children did not.

"I've got to get Christmas presents for my kids," he said urgently, nudging aside the teeth, which the imp whipped back into his mouth. "Oh, Lord. This is awful. One of them likes magic tricks, but I can't remember which. Give me seven or eight good ones. I'll send 'em to both." He drummed his fingers on the glass countertop near a pyramid of white velvet sacks labeled Winter Magic. The topmost sack tumbled off the pile and landed next to his hand.

"Okeydokey. What tricks would you like?"

"Gee, I don't know." Adam absentmindedly lifted up the white velvet sack and began to play with the cords that held it shut. "Card tricks. Hat tricks. Whatever. You pick 'em out for me, okay? Just make sure they're not too hard—but not too easy either. My kids are both smart," he challenged as though he thought he was about to be contradicted.

The imp's blue eyes flashed traffic-light green. "Yes, sir. We aim to please, sir. My wish is your command, sir." Leaping over the counter in one bound, he flew across the room and in whirlwind fashion began to pull things off the shelves. "Fixed deck of cards. Top hat with stuffed bunny. Floating light bulb. Severed finger. Flying kidneys. Levitating the baby-sitter. Sawing the principal in half." The imp plopped everything in front of Adam. "There you go, sir. Seven good tricks—not too hard, not too easy—for your delightfully eggheaded children. Will that be all?"

"Yes. I guess so." He glanced down at the sack. It was unfastened. "Uh, and this too. Whatever it is."

The imp took it from him and, without bothering to retie the cords, added it to the pile. "A good choice." He winked. His eyeball boinged out of its socket and snapped back in again, as if on a spring.

Adam didn't notice. He was taking out his wallet. "How much?" he asked.

"Seven thousand one hundred ninety dollars and sixty-five cents," the imp answered immediately.

4

"Huh?"

"Seventeen ninety-five," the imp amended.

"Really? That's cheap."

"Christmas special, sir."

Adam took out a twenty. "What about shipping?"

"Shipping?"

"Mailing and handling. Express. To California."

"Ah, your children live in California."

"That's right." Adam looked down at his wallet. Two pictures were sticking out of it. He didn't remember pulling them out. Even though he was in a hurry and he thought the salesman somewhat strange, he found himself handing the photos to the imp. "That's Danny and that's Laura," he said proudly.

"Danny and Laura. Laura and Danny," the imp repeated, as if memorizing the names. "Danny and Laura. Laura and Danny."

Adam thought the imp was mocking them. "They're good kids," he defended.

Putting his chin in his hand, the imp leaned over the counter. "Good? Good how?" he asked confidentially. "Good-natured? Good-humored? Goody-goody? Good-for-nothing?"

"Just good," Adam answered, confused and annoyed.

"Why'd you send them to California, then?"

"I didn't send them to California." Adam was getting upset. "It was Ginny's—their mother's—idea. First she left me, then she left Vermont."

"Sounds like a good idea to me."

"What does?"

"Leaving Vermont."

5

"Look. I have a job here. I spent years building up my clientele. I couldn't just . . ." Suddenly there was a sound behind him. The sound of door chimes. Adam broke off and blinked. "What . . . what's the time?" He shook himself and looked at his watch. "Two fifteen! Oh, man, I've got an appointment in fifteen minutes. Look, can you ship these or not?" He glanced up.

There was no one there.

"What the heck . . ." Adam Pauling whirled around.

A woman, tall and stately, stood there in the doorway. "May I help you?" she asked, crossing the room.

"Where's the guy?" he asked.

"Pardon?"

"The guy. The salesclerk. He was here just a moment ago."

The woman, who was Lydia Rivera, the shop's proprietor, gave him a puzzled but indulgent look as she gracefully doffed and hung up her coat. "We have no male personnel here, only myself and my daughter. She should have been waiting on you . . . Rosie!" she called into the back room.

"I tell you there was a guy here. Funny-looking guy. Wild hair. Odd eyes. Electric blue."

Lydia frowned. "Another customer, perhaps?" she said.

"Thief, more likely," Adam said, looking down at the twenty still clutched in his hand.

"Oh, dear. Really? I'll call the police at once."

"No. He didn't take anything. Not of mine, anyway. Listen, I'm in a hurry. Add this up fast, will ya?" He gestured at the merchandise.

Lydia did a quick calculation. "One hundred twenty dollars and eighty-seven cents," she said as she deftly tied the cords of the sack atop the man's pile of gifts.

Adam clicked his tongue in frustration. He didn't have enough cash. He'd have to give the woman his credit card and that would take extra time. But he wasn't about to leave without the gifts. No matter what his ex-wife, Ginny, thought, he wasn't a bad father. He cared about his kids. It was just that there was never enough time . . .

"Would you like this wrapped and shipped anywhere?" Lydia asked at last, handing him the credit-card slip she'd just made out for his signature. "I'll just need the address and these greeting cards filled out."

"No, that's okay," he answered brusquely, scrawling his name across the paper. "I'll send the stuff myself." Before Lydia could utter another word, he scooped up the packages and charged out the door.

Lydia stared after him, confused and annoyed. What was that all about? What's going on? she wondered. A quick look around the shop showed nothing out of order. She checked the cash register. All the money seemed to be there. She'd have to ask Rosie, though. It had been her turn to count the cash this morning. Rosie. Where is that girl? Lydia asked herself. "Rosie!" she called again, as she walked into the back room. "Rose! Rosamunde!"

"I'm down here, Mom," her daughter's newly restored voice rose thinly from somewhere beneath her feet.

"Oh, really? And what are you doing down there? Hiding from the customers?" Lydia shouted, crossing to the basement door.

"I'm not hiding."

"That's good to know. Then you can come up here. At once."

"No, I can't."

"Can't? What do you mean you can't?"

"I'm kind of . . . tied up at the moment." Rosie's nervous giggle drifted up the stairs.

"Rosamunde Rivera, I'm going to throttle you." Lydia threw open the door with a bang and stomped down the steps. But when she reached the bottom and saw her daughter, she gasped.

"Rosie! Oh, God, Rosie! What happened? Who did this to you?" she demanded, as she rushed over and began to untie her daughter's bonds.

"Well, uh . . ."

"A thief! There *was* a thief! That customer said there was. Nothing seems to be stolen or damaged, though."

"Really?" Rosie gawked. "No damage? Nothing broken?"

"Nothing I could see. But it must have been a thief. . . . Unless he himself . . . My God! We'll have to call the police. You'll have to give a description of the man who did this. What did he look like?"

"Well, uh . . ."

"You did see him, didn't you?"

"Well, um, yes—and no."

"What do you mean, yes and no?"

"I mean . . . Ouch!" Rosie complained, as her mother's fingers, busily working the knots, pinched her. "Please be careful, Mom."

A moment later, Lydia finished. Rosie stood up and

stretched. Then her mother took her by the shoulders and stared into her face. Rosie tried to look away but found she couldn't. "Rosie. My own, my darling, Rose," said Lydia through gritted teeth. "Tell your mother, who loves you very, very much, was there or wasn't there a thief?"

"Well, not exactly."

"Who was there exactly?" Lydia roared.

"*What* is more like it," Rosie muttered.

"What did you say?"

Wordlessly, Rosie bent behind a bench, picked up an empty glass bottle, and handed it to her mother.

Lydia looked at the label. "*Impus mischievous,*" she read, "*Variety: Nuisance. Captured at Port Sulphur, Plaquemines Parish, Louisiana, 1928.*" Lydia's flushed cheeks paled. "Oh no," she moaned. "Oh no." She began to pace and wring her hands. Then she bit her lip and paced some more. But suddenly, she stopped and took a deep breath. "We must stay calm," she said.

"Calm," Rosie repeated.

"We must be practical."

"Practical."

"Where is it now? You saw it. That man saw it. But it disappeared when I came into the shop. Did it come down here?" she blurted.

"No. No, I don't think so."

"It must be here somewhere. Imps can only vanish by entering an open container of some sort. A bottle. A vase. A sack."

"Well, there's plenty of all of those around," Rosie sighed.

"I'm afraid you're absolutely right," her mother said.

"So, let's get going. We have to close, cork, and tie everything in sight—if it takes all day, which it probably will. And then . . ." She paused.

"And then?" her daughter asked, wide eyed.

"And then, Rosie Rivera, we cross our fingers and pray."

Chapter Two

"Dashing through the snow
In a one-horse open sleigh,
O'er the fields we go
Laughing all the way . . ."

Danny Pauling, age twelve, rose on one elbow and flicked sand from his beach towel at the radio. The music faded. Danny gave a satisfied grunt, which turned into a groan when a cheery voice boomed out:

"Ha-ha-ha-happy holidays to all you cool folk listening to WHOT. This is your friend Barry Blend. It's ten forty-five on this beautiful Saturday morning, and the temperature is a holly jolly seventy-two degrees. Get ready for another very merry day at the beach—if you're not already there—"

"Shut up, will ya?" Danny growled, and tossed a whole handful of sand at the boom box.

"Don't do that, Danny. It's bad for the speakers," said his sister, Laura, who was two years younger in age, light-years ahead in electronics. "Just shut it off."

"What a good idea! Why didn't I think of that?" Danny reached out and pushed a button.

"And don't be mean," said Laura, pouring a cup of lemonade from a thermos.

"Sorry," Danny mumbled. He was silent for a moment. Then he sat up and blurted, "The sun's shining. It's seventy-two degrees. We're lying on the beach. What's wrong with this picture? Nothing, if it were July. But it's December! One week till Christmas! Pathetic."

Laura nodded, her brief irritation changing to sympathy. "I know. At home it's probably thirty degrees."

"Maybe only twenty. And there's got to be snow. Lots of it."

"And ice. On the pond. We could be skating."

"Yeah. Or sledding. Or just having hot chocolate in front of the fireplace." Danny glanced at Laura's cup with distaste. She frowned and poured the liquid out on the sand. "Why the heck did we have to move to L.A.?" Danny grumbled.

Laura didn't reply. She didn't need to. Danny knew the answer as well as she did. They both remembered the day six months ago when their mother announced, "There's no town around here we can move to that isn't on your father's route. Every time he passes through he'll be using our place as a motel. Besides, I'm sick to death of New England winters. Pack your cutoffs and sandals and give those parkas to Goodwill. We're heading west, gang. Far, far west."

Danny and Laura, especially Danny, had tried to argue, but it did no good. It took Ginny Pauling a long time to make up her mind. But once she did, it was made up for keeps. Besides, Danny thought then and now, who ever listens to kids?

They glanced over at their mother. She was standing near the water, looking up at a sea gull, smoothing back her short, fair windblown hair, and smiling.

"Face it. She really likes it here," said Laura.

"I know," Danny had to agree.

"Dad wouldn't like it here."

"Maybe we should go live with him."

"Where? In the Days End? The Sunrise Suites? The Happy Hunting Hotel?"

"It might be fun."

"Yeah, for about a week. Then we'd go stir-crazy."

"Yeah, I guess . . . ," Laura shrugged. "Besides, Mom would miss us if we went."

They looked over at her again. She was talking to a tall, blond well-muscled man. Ginny Pauling was thirty-three, looked ten years younger, and knew it. She'd had a couple of boyfriends since the divorce. None of them had lasted, but it didn't seem to bother her.

"She would?" murmured Danny, feeling the same painful embarrassment he always did when his mom flirted with anybody. He felt anger, too, though he didn't quite understand it. He lay back down on the towel without another word.

A moment later, Laura did the same.

They were pretending to be asleep when Ginny came over to them with the man in tow. She called their names. When they didn't open their eyes, she began to tickle their feet. Laura wasn't terribly ticklish, but Danny was hopeless. He sputtered, thrashed, and scrambled to his knees, arms up, ready to defend himself against any further attacks. A few years ago he would have attacked back. Ginny was nearly as ticklish as he was, and it used to be fun to make her squeal. But he was too old for that now. His mother knew it, and he felt doubly annoyed with her, both for playing a one-sided game and for making him look ridiculous in front of a stranger.

If Ginny knew he was irritated, she ignored it. "Danny, Laura, I want you to meet Biff. He works in the same building I do. We run into each other sometimes in the hall."

"And today we ran into each other at the beach," Biff drawled, with a hint of a Southern accent. It was a very pleasant accent. The man's smile was pleasant too—relaxed and genuine.

But it didn't endear him to Danny. "Isn't it amazing with all that running into each other you're not all black-and-blue?" he muttered.

Laura snickered. Biff's smile changed. It was now less relaxed and more wry. "A comic, eh?" he said.

"You could call him that," Ginny replied dryly. She gave Danny a warning look. "Biff has to do some Christmas shopping. So do I, and I figured you might want to do some as well. He's suggested we all go together."

"I've already finished my shopping," Danny answered flatly.

"I have, too," put in Laura, moving a little closer to her brother.

"Oh. Well, just keep us company, then. I could use your magic touch with Grandma's gift, Laura. And Danny, Biff has a son your age. You could help him pick out something for him."

"Yeah, I sure could use the help," Biff seconded. "When I was twelve, I liked country music and paleontology. As far as I can tell, my kid isn't interested in either. But it's hard for me to guess what he does like—especially since he lives with his mother in Atlanta and I don't get to see him that much."

"Danny's dad had that problem even when we all lived together. When Danny was five, Adam got him a construction set so complicated he himself couldn't put it together. Another time he gave him five books on football, when Danny was only interested in Little League. Last year he bought Laura earrings with wires—and her ears aren't pierced. God knows what he'll come up with this year," Ginny snorted. Then she looked at her kids. "So, what do you think? Shall we all go?"

Danny shook his head. "No. You can go. Laura and I want to hang out here."

"Are you sure you won't mind if I go?" Ginny looked concerned.

"We won't mind," said Laura. "You can use your own magic touch for Grandma's gift."

"Oh, all right." She shouldered her beach bag and said to Biff, "Let me go home and change. Our house is nearby. . . . See you two later."

"Nice kids," Biff said, as the two of them sauntered away. He was slightly bowlegged.

As soon as they were out of sight, Laura got up and started mimicking his walk.

Danny laughed. It made him feel a little better. Then he said, "What do you think Dad *will* send us this year? A G.I. Joe for me? A doll that poops in its diaper for you?"

"Maybe he'll send you a nice sweater that's only two sizes too small," suggested Laura.

"Maybe he'll send you a bra."

Laura swatted at him. But Danny ducked. They laughed again. "Well, maybe he'll surprise us this year and send us something really special," she said.

"Right," said Danny. "And maybe there'll be a blizzard in Beverly Hills."

"Stranger things have happened," Laura intoned, imitating their mother's voice.

Danny grunted and turned the radio back on.

Chapter Three

Twelve hours after he left Lydia Rivera's magic shop, Adam Pauling was having a bad dream. It was a dream he'd had before. It always began peacefully, with Adam and his family floating on a big white cloud. Laura had a radio that played celestial music. Danny was dangling a fishing pole over the side. Ginny nibbled at an ice-cream cone. She offered Adam a lick.

"No. I don't like bean sprouts," he replied this time (sometimes it was "I don't like raw fish"). Then he asked, "Where is this cloud going anyway?"

"California," answered Ginny.

"California! I don't want to go to California. I *can't* go to California!"

"Oh, that's too bad," Ginny said. "*We* can."

And suddenly, Adam was standing alone on a mountaintop, while the cloud carrying his family drifted farther and farther away. "No! Come back! Ginny, come back! Danny! Laura!"

"Grab hold of my line, Dad!" yelled Danny. He flipped his pole and cast the line hard.

Adam reached for it and missed. And his family kept floating away until they were no more than a dark speck in the vast blue sky.

"Come back! Please, come back!" Adam kept shouting until he woke up, with his cheeks wet and his throat dry.

He sat up in bed, disoriented. Flicking on the bedside lamp, he squinted around trying to figure out where he was. Another sleep factory, he thought at last, taking in the motel's bland beige carpeting, the flat green walls, the bad reproduction of a bad painting over a dull cream-colored bureau.

Then his eyes landed on the pile of gifts, along with wrapping paper, ribbons, and such, sitting on one of the room's two regulation tan chairs. For a moment he couldn't figure out what they were. Then he remembered the magic shop and the weird salesman—or thief, or whatever he was. Did I really show him pictures of my kids? Adam wondered. He shook his head and yawned.

He knew from experience he was not about to fall back asleep. Getting out of bed, he stretched, rubbed his eyes, and sat down in the other chair to begin wrapping his children's gifts.

Across town, Rosie Rivera was also awake. Overtired from all the work of sealing every item in the store to prevent the imp's reappearance, as well as from her encounter with the creature, she lay in bed in the dark, fidgeting and pulling at the loose threads of her blanket.

But now she wasn't thinking of the imp. She was thinking about Johnny Haines, or rather something Lydia had suggested in reference to him. It was after Rosie had confessed to her mother about the love potion and then complained about Lydia's lack of instruction in the fine art of witchcraft.

"I don't understand why you've given it up. At the very least, we could use some magic to bring some customers into this place," Rosie complained.

Lydia grew very serious then. "I believe I've said this to you before, Rosie. It's more satisfying to achieve success by using means other than magic—more satisfying and, as you've now seen for yourself, safer."

"Yeah, and it's more satisfying to achieve success than failure—by any means," Rosie grumbled.

"Look," said Lydia. "Why don't you call up this boy and wish him a Merry Christmas? Maybe even invite him over sometime for a mug of hot cider. The worst he can say is no."

"And tell all his friends and have everybody laugh at me behind my back," Rosie retorted.

"Why would they laugh?" Lydia looked truly puzzled.

Rosie sighed. In some ways her mother was extremely sophisticated. She certainly *looked* sophisticated, with her perfect posture and her glossy dark hair always neatly bobbed. But in other ways, such as understanding teenage social affairs, she was totally naive. Oh, Lydia, Rosie wanted to explain, because Johnny Haines—or the Jack of Hearts, as he's called—is one of the most popular guys in junior high. While I, on the other hand, am known as Houdini's Daughter, and none of them would care if I did a vanishing act. But she chose not to say that to her mother. Instead, she just said, "Mom, when you were my age, would you have called up a guy you liked who didn't like you?"

"Yes," Lydia replied. "That's how I met your father."

"I should have guessed." Rosie chuckled and smiled affectionately at her mother.

Lydia smiled back. Then she said, "Call him up, Rosie. You might be pleasantly surprised at what happens."

"I'll think about it," Rosie had said.

And so she was. She was imagining what would happen if she really did call the Jack of Hearts and he was actually happy to hear from her. Maybe he'd ask her out. Maybe they could go skating or on a romantic walk by Copper Lake.

She pictured them standing by the water, tossing bread to the ducks, chatting merrily, or perhaps silently enjoying each other's company. They'd stand there, not quite looking at one another, his gloved hand just brushing her sleeve. Rosie sighed, drifting into that pleasant twilight state prior to sleep.

He tosses the last handful of bread into the water and dusts his hands. He turns to me. I turn to him. And yes, he is going to kiss me. I close my eyes and raise my chin, waiting, waiting.

Smack, smack come loud disgusting smooch noises. My

eyes fly open. There, instead of Johnny Haines, is the imp.

"Not again!" Rosie yelled, sitting bolt upright, opening her eyes for real, and turning on the light.

But when she looked around, there was nobody there. She leapt out of bed and double-checked every container in her room where the imp might hide. They were all sealed shut. "Ugh!" She shook herself the way a dog sheds water. "Ugh and double ugh!"

Throwing open the window, she stuck her head out, breathed in the cold air, and wished upon the first bright star she noticed (Betelgeuse, as a matter of fact) that the imp was truly gone for good.

Chapter Four

Danny was lying on his bed, conducting an imaginary interview with himself. "We're here at the Pauling residence on Christmas Day to ask Danny Pauling how he's enjoying his holiday," he announced into his fist as if it were a microphone. "Well, Danny, how do you like Christmas in L.A.?"

"It sucks," Danny replied to himself. "It reeks. It bites the big one. I wish that America would eliminate Christmas. I wish that America would eliminate California!"

"Well, Danny, it seems you're having 'a little trouble adjusting to your new environment,'" he quoted his science teacher on his last report card.

"Aw, why don't you blow it out of your ear, you . . ."

"Danny?" Laura called, rapping on his closed door. She'd been waiting for hours for him to come downstairs.

Patient Laura, she thought. That's what everyone calls me. In third grade she'd even won an award for it. Well, she was tired of being patient now. "Danny," she repeated, "are you awake yet?"

"No," he replied.

"Do you know what time it is?"

"Pacific standard time," he answered, knowing it would bug her. He didn't particularly want to annoy his sister, but sometimes he couldn't seem to help it.

Laura sighed. She'd thought Danny might act weird today, but she didn't think he'd act this weird. It *was* strange, celebrating their first Christmas without their father, on another perfect beach day in California, yet. Laura was hoping she and Danny could help each other get through it, maybe even enjoy it. It bothered her that since they'd moved there, her brother was such an inconsistent ally. Sometimes he was her best friend; other times he acted almost like a stranger.

"Well, are you planning to wake up soon?" she demanded. "I want to open my presents."

"So, who's stopping you?"

"You are!" she shouted.

Whoa, Danny thought, startled. Laura hardly ever yelled. She made him feel guilty and selfish. He padded slowly to the door and opened it. He was wearing jeans and a long-sleeved flannel shirt, the same shirt he'd worn last Christmas in Vermont. Now it was a little too tight and a lot too warm. His eyes defied her to comment on it, but she didn't say a word. He sniffed the air. "What's that smell?"

"Waffles," she answered.

"Mom's making waffles?" Danny's eyebrows went up. He didn't want to seem pleased, or even surprised, but he couldn't help it. He loved waffles, and Ginny hadn't made them in a long time.

"Yes. She said she wanted to make us a special breakfast—except now it's more like lunch," Laura said pointedly.

"Yeah. Okay," Danny muttered, by way of apology. Brushing past Laura, he went downstairs.

Ginny was singing "Hark! The Herald Angels Sing" loudly and off-key as she spooned batter onto the waffle iron. Unnoticed, Danny stood watching her. She looks happy, he said to himself. Her first Christmas without Dad and she's happy. It isn't right.

Unbidden, an image sprang into his head of last Christmas. It hadn't started off badly. Dad was home and telling a lot of corny jokes, which Danny secretly enjoyed. Mom was cooking and taking photographs.

Then came the game. It was called Honesty. Just a dumb board game that their aunt Jackie had sent them.

The question Dad had to answer was: "The most important thing in the world to me is . . ." Mom was supposed to guess what he'd written down before he showed it to anyone. "My job," she said immediately.

Dad held up his pad. On it was written, "My family." Mom read the words aloud as if they were the funniest joke Dad had told all day. Then she looked at him and said, "I thought this game was called Honesty, not Horse Manure."

Danny remembered Laura looking at him, her eyes

saying, How big a fight will this one be? How long before we have to leave the room? He'd grabbed his pad of paper and written down, "5 minutes." Laura held up hers. It said, "2 minutes." When they left they looked at their watches. Laura had won.

Well, it still isn't right, Danny thought now, looking at his mother, missing his father. She shouldn't be happy. But much as he tried to convince himself that this was so, he wasn't totally sure—and that made him feel guilty, which made him feel worse.

Then Ginny looked up and saw him. She didn't comment on his choice of clothing either. But she did tease, "Hey, kiddo. I see you made it down before New Year's." Then she came around the corner and hugged him. "Merry Christmas. What do you want first, eats or treats?" She opened the iron to show him a golden brown waffle.

Danny's stomach growled. "I guess I got my answer," said Ginny.

Behind them Laura groaned.

They turned and looked at her.

"Why can't we have both at the same time?" she asked.

"Well, why not?" Ginny waved her spoon like a magic wand.

Soon after, they were sitting in the living room opening presents between bites of breakfast. Danny was still trying to maintain his bad mood, but it was getting hard. Laura and Ginny had given him such good presents. A 1954 Boston Red Sox hat and a Carl Yastrzemski baseball card, among other things. When he found himself feeling too enthusiastic, he'd turn and stare at the tacky little white Christmas tree his mother had put up the night before.

"We agreed not to spend the money on a real tree this year. So I decided if we had to get a fake, I'd get the fakey-est fake around. I'd say this fills the bill, wouldn't you?" She seemed to find the thing amusing. Danny found it depressing. Mom and Dad may have argued, but at least there was enough money when he was around to buy a real tree, he thought.

"So," he said, swallowing the last bit of his waffle. "Are we finished now?"

"No. You haven't opened your father's gifts yet," Ginny told him.

"Why bother?" he muttered.

"Come on, Danny. Be a good sport for a change," she replied.

"You made fun of his gifts last week to that bowlegged bozo, Barf."

"Biff," Ginny said. "And I think that passing remarks about someone's physical appearance is really scummy, Danny."

He reddened, knowing perfectly well she was right. "Well, anyway, you did," he said, after a moment's silence.

"Maybe he's done a better job this year," Ginny said. "Or . . ."

"Or what?"

"Or if he hasn't, we can *all* make fun of them," suggested Laura.

She and Ginny giggled and even Danny's lips twitched. He and Laura pulled out the big box lying under the tree and tore off the wrapping.

Laura riffled through it and read the labels off some of

the small packages she found inside. "Crazy Aces, the Severed Finger. Ew, gross."

But Danny's eyes lit up. "Hey, they're magic tricks. Keenola!"

Laura grinned. Danny hadn't used "Paulingese," their special slang, in years. It meant he was really pleased. He looked up at her, suddenly self-conscious. "Where's your present from Dad?" he asked gruffly. "All I see are these tricks."

"I guess they're for both of us," she answered graciously, brushing aside her own disappointment to encourage her brother's enthusiasm. It was important to her that he be happy. When he wasn't, his bad mood clung to her like chewing gum on the heel of a shoe.

"It figures," said Danny. "He couldn't remember which of us liked magic."

"It doesn't matter." Laura shrugged. "You can learn the tricks. I can be your assistant. I'm really good at smiling a lot." She flashed a huge toothy grin.

Danny started laughing. So did Ginny. Then the phone rang. Ginny went to answer it.

Danny opened the Floating Light Bulb and started reading the instructions. They were easy to follow. In less than a minute, he'd mastered the trick.

"Maybe Dad didn't do such a bad job this year after all," said Laura.

Danny humphed begrudgingly in agreement. He took out the Magical Handkerchief and was trying to learn it when Ginny came into the room.

"Who was it, Mom?" Laura asked. "Was it Dad?"

Ginny shook her head. "He'll probably call later. Smack in the middle of dinner, no doubt."

A moment went by before Laura realized her mother hadn't answered her first question. "So, who did call?" she repeated.

Ginny picked a piece of lint off her dress. "Biff," she replied. "He's lonely. It's Christmas, and he misses his son." She seemed to be holding back something.

Laura waited warily. She sensed that her mother was about to smash the fragile comfort and joy they were having.

"He's a nice guy," Ginny announced defensively. "And I know how he feels. So I invited him over. Or, more specifically, he invited himself over, and I said okay."

"Oh, Mom, you didn't," Laura rapped out.

Danny's eyes, cloudy with concentration, looked up from his trick. "What's going on?" he queried, blinking.

Ginny's lips tightened. She looked ready for a fight. "Biff is coming over to have some eggnog with us."

Danny blinked again, chasing out of his head phrases such as "Slip the thumb tip over your finger" and "Direct the audience's attention to the silk," and tried to understand what his mother had just said. "Biff? He's coming here? When?"

"In an hour."

"What?" Danny's voice was like a cat's growl. All the good feelings he'd been allowing himself to have fled, and the bad rushed back in. "You said you wanted to spend Christmas alone with us. You made a big deal out of it. 'It'll be just the three of us,' you said. 'No Cousin Tina to eat all the candy. No Uncle Mike to get drunk and sing dirty songs. . . .'" Danny's voice was still low, but his

28

cheeks were red and his eyes were blazing. "And no Dad. No Dad to tell dumb jokes. To play football with the cushions. To have a big screaming fight with until Laura and I can't stand it anymore and we have to run out of the room." His voice rose, and so did he. "God, I hate Christmas. I hate this place. I hate you!" He grabbed a white velvet sack from the box of tricks and reared back to fling it at his mother.

"Danny!" Laura yelled.

He stopped, lowering his arm. Then he turned and ran out the door.

It wasn't until half an hour later that Laura found him sitting hunched under the pier. He had something in his hand. The white velvet sack, she saw when she got close enough. He was dangling it by its silver cords, spinning slow circles above the sand.

She sat down next to him. He didn't say anything. "You're not going to throw that at me, are you?" she said lightly.

He didn't reply, just kept twirling the sack.

"Mom acts really stupid sometimes, doesn't she?"

Danny still remained silent. Now he was jiggling the sack, making it dance in the air.

Laura reached out and took it away from him. "Winter Magic," she read. "Good trick?"

"I don't know," he replied hoarsely.

She undid the knot and opened the sack. She peered inside for instructions but couldn't find any. What she did see was a bit of silver. She pulled it. A glittering lacy snowflake emerged, followed by a second and a third. Still she kept pulling. More and more snowflakes appeared, each attached to the next, an impossible number it seemed for such a small sack. She smiled. It was a one-time-only trick, but it was a cute one.

When she'd tugged out the last snowflake, she draped the chain around her neck and laid down the sack.

Danny looked at it. "Winter Magic," he sniffed. "I wish I had some magic. Some power to do things. To change things. To make whatever I want come true."

It was at precisely that moment when the smoke began to pour from the white velvet sack. To pour and swirl and spiral up and up in a column beneath the pier.

Laura saw it first, and she gasped. Danny saw it and gulped. They both watched in awe as a tall, skinny figure with crazy hair, electric blue eyes, and large teeth stepped out of the smoke, smiled, and declared, "Hello, hello, hello, Danny and Laura. Your wish, my dear liberators, is my command."

Danny and Laura shouted and scrambled backward in the sand. They didn't hear the imp, still smiling, murmur, "That is until I have something better to do." They had started to run away.

The imp made a slight gesture with his hand, and Danny and Laura found they could no longer move. They whimpered in fear. "Don't worry. That's just until you take it easy," he said. Then, throwing wide his arms, he sang a stirring rendition of "California, Here I Come," bowed three times, and waited patiently for Danny and Laura to calm down.

Chapter Five

The dishes were washed. The roaster remains were wrapped and refrigerated. And Rosie Rivera, trying hard not to stare at the telephone, was doing an unintentional impersonation of Frankenstein's monster singing "Have Yourself a Merry Little Christmas."

"Rosie, for heaven's sake!" Lydia hollered from the kitchen, where she was heating up some cider.

Rosie frowned and stopped roaring and grunting. What a rotten Christmas, she thought. The worst since the one after Dad split a jillion years ago.

First of all, they were broke. The big Christmas rush she and her mother had hoped for had not materialized. It seemed more likely than ever that Lydia would have to close the store and that they would maybe even move out of town.

If we move out of town, I'll never see Johnny Haines again, thought Rosie. Not ever. Not that it matters—at least not to Johnny Haines. She turned and stared at the phone after all, begging it to ring.

That was the second thing that had made this Christmas crummy. That darn phone call. She had finally made it. That very morning. What the heck, she'd told herself. So what if he, they, all laugh at me. They laugh anyway, no matter what I do. Then she'd picked up the phone and dialed Johnny's number. His mother had answered. When Rosie asked for Johnny, Mrs. Haines said that he was out skating and would be back in an hour or so.

"Would you like to leave a message?" she'd asked.

Rosie had taken a deep breath and said, "Yes. Yes. Tell him Rosie Rivera called to wish him a Merry Christmas. If he'd like to wish her one back, he can call her at 555-4321." Then she'd hung up, fast.

All day she'd attempted to forget about the call. But it hadn't worked. It had been all she could think about. Now it was nearly five o'clock, and Johnny still hadn't phoned. Maybe he never got the message, she tried to convince herself. Maybe he broke his ankle skating and they had to take him to the hospital and he's sitting there with a cast on his leg. Maybe he had a close encounter with my friend the imp. . . .

Rosie grimaced. She'd managed to put the creature out of her mind for a while, and she didn't care to remember him now. "Well, at least *he* won't give us any more trouble," she said aloud.

"Who won't give us any more trouble?" asked Lydia, entering the room with two steaming mugs.

"The imp," Rosie said, a little sheepishly. She didn't want to keep reminding her mother of her blunder if she could help it.

"Ah" was all Lydia said. The truth was she felt far less confident than her daughter. There was something niggling in the back of her mind regarding the imp. But for the life of her she couldn't remember what it was.

Rosie looked at her quizzically. Lydia handed her a mug and settled down with her own in the big overstuffed armchair.

"You *are* sure he's gone, aren't you?" Rosie asked.

"Well, he hasn't reappeared in seven days, and that's a good sign. Unrestrained imps cannot stay hidden for long. It's not in their nature." Though Lydia had tried to sound confident, Rosie detected her mother's unspoken concern.

"But . . . ," she prompted.

"But . . . ," Lydia began. Then she frowned and gave a nearly imperceptible twitch. "But let's not go poking around any more items in the basement, right?"

Although she knew her mother was still within her rights to scold her, Rosie found herself getting annoyed. Items in the basement indeed. She remembered the day Lydia had bought the shop from old Mr. Melchior, a strange fish if there ever was one. "There are some items in the basement you may find useful one day," he'd said, and he'd handed her an inventory, which included a set of pretty amulets, minus their instructions; several dusty volumes of spells; a motley assortment of bottles, baskets, and lamps; and an empty brown bag that always produced lunch. They were all still down there, undusted and untouched.

"I don't get it," Rosie said now, in a cross voice. "You tell me you don't want to practice witchcraft anymore. You say it's better to get things without resorting to magic. Well, then how come you've kept all that stuff that's in the basement?"

"I've told you, Rosie. It's not so easy to . . . *dispose* of that 'stuff.' If it got into the wrong hands . . . well, you should have a pretty good idea by now of what might happen," Lydia answered.

"And what about the other items? The herbs, the unguents, the things you use to cast spells. Don't tell me it's hard to get rid of those, too. Why don't you just dump them down the toilet if you're not going to use them?"

Lydia's olive skin flushed slightly. She turned the big silver ring—the only piece of jewelry she wore—around and around on her finger, signaling to Rosie that she was getting annoyed, too.

But Rosie persisted. "Come on, Mom. Be honest. You know you want to be a witch again. You know it. It's in your blood. And it's in mine, too. If you'd teach me, I could do things properly and not mess up like I did with the imp. Come on, Mom. Say you'll do it. Give me a Christmas present to remember!"

Lydia stopped turning the ring and gazed at her daughter. For a moment Rosie thought she saw her eyes soften. Then, straightening the high and rather severe collar of her cotton blouse, Lydia commanded, "Drink your cider, Rosamunde, before it gets cold."

Oooh, Rosie gritted her teeth in frustration—and also

in silence. Her mother's cool stare wouldn't let her say another word.

And then the phone rang.

Rosie jumped, and then jumped up. "Oh, my God. Oh, my God," she babbled. "I'll get it. I'll get it. And could you, um, uh . . ."

"Of course," Lydia said. Relieved to be finished with the conversation, she discreetly left the room.

Rosie grabbed hold of the phone. "Oh, my God," she muttered again, and let it ring once more before she lifted up the receiver. She took a deep breath. "Hello," she said at last, in the smoothest, most sophisticated tone she could muster. "Rivera residence. Rosie Rivera speaking."

"Well, hi. Howdy. How are ya? *Bonjour. Buenos días.* Good morning. Good afternoon. Goodness gracious, great balls of fire!" a voice boomed.

Rosie held the receiver away from her ear and grimaced. Then she said, "Who is this?"

"You don't recognize me? Golly gee, I'm hurt, crushed, cut up, crestfallen, pierced to the heart, wounded to the quick."

"Who *is* this?" Rosie insisted, a bit quaveringly. There was something familiar about the voice . . . something unnervingly familiar.

"On the other hand," it went on, "I guess we didn't really have much of a conversation. You were kind of tied up at the time. Anyway, I called to say the weather's fine, wish you were here, having a great time, everything's coming up roses, life is just a bowl of cherries. And, oh yes, thanks. If it hadn't been for you, I'd never have popped

35

my cork. If you ever head out this way, be sure to look me up. As for *locking* me up again—sweetheart, don't even try. . . . Well, toodle-oo, and may all your wishes turn blue." Click. The phone went dead.

For a long moment, Rosie just stood there, staring at the receiver. Then suddenly she began to giggle. Not a cheery giggle, but a high-pitched, teeth-chattering one.

Lydia heard it all the way out in the kitchen, and she hurried into the room. "Rosie? Rosie! What is it? Who was it? What's going on?"

Rosie kept laughing until suddenly she just stopped. "*Who* was it?" she said, eyes wide and glassy with shock. "Try *what?*"

"What? What do you mean? What just happened?"

"He's got quite a peculiar sense of humor, doesn't he?"

"*Who? What*, for heaven's sake?" Lydia shouted.

Rosie took a deep breath and shuddered. "The imp," she said.

Lydia turned pale. "The imp? He just called you? Where is he?"

"I don't know. He didn't say exactly."

"Well, we have to find out. At once."

"Why? What difference will it make?"

"He's got enough power on his own. But if he attaches himself to someone, if he gets into someone's house and links up with that person's energy, his power could double or triple," Lydia explained.

"But what can we do about it?" Rosie stared at her mother.

What she saw cleared her head. Lydia's eyes gleamed

as though they were lit up from the inside, and the look they bore was one of total and fearsome determination. "It's time to dust off my book of spells, unpack my cauldron, and grind up some herbs," she announced.

"You mean . . ."

"Yes. I mean it's time once again to take up the Craft."

Rosie felt a thrill shoot through her. "I'll help you," she responded ardently.

"You bet you will," Lydia declared unequivocally, and, taking the receiver out of her daughter's hand, she firmly hung up the phone.

Chapter Six

So, what's *your* name?" Laura asked the imp as he turned from the telephone booth on the pier. "What do we call *you?*" She was holding her brother's hand, and he was letting her—a sure sign that, though their initial shock had worn off, they were still more than a little stunned. A second sign was that it did not strike either of them as comical or unusual that a genie would need to use the telephone.

"Let's see . . . ," said the imp, running his hands through the great bush of brassy blond hair that sprang in all directions from his scalp. It immediately grew another six inches in height.

He looks like a cartoon character who stuck his finger in a socket, Laura thought, not knowing if that impression made her more wary of the creature or less.

"I've always been partial to the name Amenhotep myself," he finished.

"Amenhotep? He was an Egyptian pharaoh," Danny spoke up.

"True. Two people can have the same name, though. There's more than one Danny and Laura, wouldn't you say? However, since you object—and I most certainly don't want to offend my hosts, who were so kind as to release me from that sack—you can call me Mr. Ed instead."

Laura let out a giggle. But Danny didn't even crack a smile. Instead he dropped Laura's hand and said, "Okay, Ed—"

"*Mr.* Ed," corrected the imp.

"Okay, *Mr.* Ed or Amenhotep or whatever your name is, let's get down to business. You said you're going to grant us our wishes, right? Like the genie in Aladdin's lamp?"

"Sure. Why not?" The imp riffled through his hair again and pulled out a fish, which he tossed off the pier. The ocean was some distance away, but the fish seemed to be of the flying variety. It soared through the air and landed in the water with only the faintest splash.

Danny ignored the interruption. "So, how many wishes do we get?" he asked baldly.

"How many?" Mr. Ed stared at him in amusement. "Oh, dozens, I'd say."

"You mean there's no limit?"

"That's right. There's no limit."

"You're kidding!" Laura exclaimed. Like her brother, she'd been expecting to hear the old "you-only-get-three-wishes" routine found in practically every fairy tale they'd ever read.

"Great," said Danny. But it wasn't a wholehearted "great." He didn't quite trust this genie. Not yet. Not until he'd proved his worth. "Then you wouldn't mind granting me one right now."

"Not in the least," said the imp. "Go ahead, kid. Tell Mr. Ed what you want for Christmas."

Danny's eyes glinted with challenge and a touch of greed. "Okay. I want a brand-new bike."

The imp's bright blue eyes drooped. His shoulders sagged. He let out a big yawn, as if he were totally, completely bored. Then he started walking up the pier.

Danny and Laura turned to watch him. He was taking his time, going nowhere in a hurry. At the far end, heading toward him, was a kid about Danny's age, taking his shiny BMX for a spin.

The imp waited until the kid was just about to pass him. Then he waggled his fingers, just the way he'd done at Danny and Laura an hour or so before. The kid and his bike froze in midpedal. The imp lifted him off his vehicle and set him on a bench like a mannequin. Then he got on the bike himself and rode it, without hands, up to Danny and Laura.

"Here you go," he said. "One brand-new bike."

"Oh, come on!" Danny jeered.

"Hey, what's the matter? You don't like this model? You one of those un-American types who only wants a Raleigh or a Peugeot or anything so long as it's not made in the U.S.A.? I'll have you know—"

"It's not the bike. It's how you got it. You stole it!"

"Listen, kid. You said you wanted a bike. You didn't say I had to pay for it."

"But you're supposed to be able to make it *appear*," Laura put in. "You know, by using magic."

"Honey, let me give you a tip—one all us genies know: 'When in doubt, take the easy way out.' Making something like a bike—all that metal and rubber—that's hard work. Why bother doing it if you don't have to?"

"Either you're the laziest genie I've ever heard of, or you're not a genie at all," Danny sneered.

"True. Maybe I'm not a genie. Maybe I'm a mirage, a delusion, a hallucination, a figment of your imagination. Maybe you've gone crazy, bonkers, loony, nuts!" The imp danced around the pier, making monkey faces and shaking peanuts out of his hair.

"Let's ask him to grant something else," Laura suggested.

"Okay. Go ahead. You try it this time."

Laura cleared her throat. "Mr. Ed?"

The imp ignored her and continued to gibber and scratch at his armpits.

"Mr. Ed!"

The imp stopped. "Yes?" he said, smiling politely.

"First of all, I want you to return that bike to that kid you took it from."

"All right." The imp sent the bike rolling down to the boy and released the kid from his spell. The boy shot him one terrified look, jumped on his bike, and burned out of there.

"Good," said Laura. "And now I want you to fix it so I can fly."

"To fly! Like our avian friends in the sky! Tasting the clouds! Drifting through the blue! Soaring through the sunlight!" the imp rhapsodized. "How beautiful! How poetic! How—"

"Are you just gonna run your mouth all day or are you going to grant her wish?" Danny interrupted.

"Impatient, aren't you?" Mr. Ed snapped at him. Danny might have been startled by the nasty expression on his face if he'd had time to see it. But before he could blink, the imp was grinning again, good-naturedly, at Laura. "You want to fly, my dear, and so you shall. So you shall."

He turned so that he was facing a small tourist shop with an elaborate display of Santa and his reindeer on its roof. Then he shook out his sleeves like a magician about to perform. "Drumroll, please," he announced. From out of nowhere came a rat-ta-tat-tat that made Danny and Laura jump. The imp pointed at Santa. "To the top of the porch! To the top of the wall! Now dash away! Dash away! Dash away . . ." He made a rude gesture at the statue. "All!"

And the statue did—fly, that is. Sled and all. Right straight at Danny and Laura.

Danny swore and ducked.

Laura shut her eyes and shielded her head. So she didn't actually see the sled's runner hook through the epaulet on her shirtsleeve and lift her by one shoulder into the air.

"Help! Help!" she shrieked, twisting and dangling above the pier, above the sand, above the Pacific Ocean. "Put me down! Put me down!"

"Oh, well. If you insist . . ." The imp made the same rude gesture at Santa, and Laura fell, kerplunk, onto the crest of a wave that washed her, coughing and sputtering, up onto the shore.

Santa and his reindeer sailed neatly back to their perch as if they'd never moved at all.

"You creep! You jerk!" Danny yelled furiously over his shoulder at the imp as he charged off the pier and across the sand to his sister. He helped her to her feet. "Are you okay? Do you hurt anywhere?"

Still wheezing, she shook her head.

He patted her back. "Let's get out of here and tell that maniac what he can do with his wishes."

They turned. The imp was standing there, blocking their way. "Don't go. I'm sorry. So very sorry. It won't happen again. I promise."

"Get out of our way," Danny growled.

"Look, we all make mistakes. Live and let live. Forgive and forget. A stitch in time saves nine—"

"I said, get out of our way!"

"Hey, I said I was sorry. What do you want me to do, kiss your feet? Well, okay, I'll kiss them." Mr. Ed dropped down, groveling at their ankles, pecking at their toes.

"Stop it! Cut it out!" Danny shouted.

Laura hiccupped and resisted the impulse to sneak a feel of the imp's amazing hair.

"Give me one more chance," the creature implored, on his knees. "Let me grant you one more wish. I guarantee this time you'll be pleased."

Danny said nothing for a moment. He was torn. On the one hand, he thought the imp could be dangerous—

or at least the way he granted wishes could be. On the other hand, if he was telling the truth now, there were all sorts of intriguing possibilities. . . . He looked at his sister for guidance. She thought for a minute and then gave a tiny nod.

He turned back to the imp. "Okay. One more chance. One. But first of all, no more 'mistakes.' You got that?"

"I got it."

"All right, then. Here's my wish. I want you to make it snow. Right here. Right now. On this very beach."

A change came over the imp then. His wild eyes lit up with sincere pleasure. His toothpaste smile turned genuine. "Weather magic? You like weather magic?" he asked.

"Uh, yeah. Sure," Danny assented, although he wasn't exactly sure what he was agreeing with.

"Me, too! It's my favorite!" the imp exclaimed, sounding very much like a happy eight-year-old boy. "I'm good at it, too. Real good. Watch. I'll show you." He stood up and stood still. The heels of his hands were pressed together, the fingers and palms were up and open. He hummed a thread of a tune under his breath, then opened his mouth and blew out a puff of silver smoke. It rose into the air, forming a dense cloud that blotted out the sun. Other clouds rolled in quickly to join it till the sky turned gray with them. Then they each gave a little shake, and a gentle snow began to descend upon the sand.

"Oh, how wonderful!" Laura burbled with delight, blinking snowflakes from her eyelashes, catching them on her tongue. "Like a crazy dream come true!"

"It is, isn't it?" the imp responded, with a proud smile. "Don't you think so, Danny?"

Eyes wide, jaw agape, Danny didn't answer. For the truth was the crazy dream that had come true was his own. That very morning in his sleep he'd stood on this very beach and watched it turn white under a blanket of snow. "Wow," he got out at last. "Double keenola!"

The imp laughed. A few moments later, he opened his mouth and inhaled. The snow ceased at once. All of the clouds dispersed, except for one, which wisped into a silver smoke that funneled down from the sky and into the imp's throat. He gave a swallow and a delicate burp. "So, I kept my word, didn't I? I granted your wish. So now you'll take me home and give me a place to stay."

"A place to stay?" Laura replied, as the imp's request sunk in. She liked him more now, and she'd been thrilled by the snow, but still, to bring him to their house?

Danny, on the other hand, did not hesitate. If the snow had not been enough to erase his doubts, the imp's blue eyes, staring fixedly at him, were. I know you, they were saying. I know what you like. We're two of a kind, you and I. Two of a kind. Together we'll do things you've only dreamed of doing. Together we'll turn this town up-side down. "Sure," Danny said. "We'll take you home with us."

"Danny, wait a minute." Laura touched his arm.

He shook her off irritably. "What is it?"

Laura was a bit surprised by his response. But then again, she was used to his mercurial moods. So, quite reasonably, she said, "I don't think that's such a great idea, bringing him to our house. First of all, he promised that he wouldn't try any funny stuff with this wish, but what about our future ones?"

"Oh, he won't try anything funny with those, either, will you?" Danny answered, dismissively.

The imp put his hand on his heart. "I do slovenly swear," he replied.

"Satisfied?" Danny asked Laura.

"I suppose. But there's another problem. What about Mom? If we bring him home, we'll have to explain him to her."

"She'll never know I'm there," the imp told her, "unless you tell her I am."

She turned to him. "You mean you can make yourself invisible?"

"No. But I can make myself scarce."

"See? There's no need to worry, Laura," Danny urged, but in a kinder tone. Laura was always more cautious than he was. He should have known better than to get on her case about it. But the snow, the dream, the imp had gotten him so excited. "It's gonna be all right. More than all right. I'll bet that snow was nothing compared to the stuff he—we'll be able to do. Right, Mr. Ed?" He grinned at the imp, who grinned back.

"You bet your life, O Danny Boy," said the creature. "We're gonna do things neither of you will ever forget, even if you try—and believe me, you will try."

"Huh?" said Laura. She wasn't sure she'd heard the imp's last six words right or, for that matter, if she'd heard his vow correctly a few moments before.

Danny hadn't heard them at all. He stood there, still smiling. Then he turned to Laura. "Any more objections, sis?" he asked in a teasing tone.

Laura looked at his flushed face and let his excitement become her own. "No, bro," she replied.

"Whoopee-ti-yi-yo! Get along little Paulings," the imp yodeled. "Go ahead and lead the way, 'cause Mr. Ed is here to stay, in sunny—or snowy—Califor-NI-ay!"

He laid his arms over Danny's and Laura's shoulders and steered them down the pier toward their house.

Chapter Seven

Flying Saucer Lands in Cornfield.' "

"Hoax."

" 'Gravestones Toppled.' That one's three days old."

"Vandalism. They finally caught the kids last night."

" 'Skies Rain Blood.' "

"Natural occurrence."

"Huh?" Rosie turned from the chart hanging on the living room wall and looked at her mother. "Since when is bloody rain a natural occurrence?"

"When a tornado whips through a tomato-juice cannery," Lydia replied. "I called there this morning."

Rosie nodded and crossed off the item on the chart. It had been her idea, this chart. When Lydia had mentioned that the imp might do newsworthy crazy stuff, she'd suggested that they keep track of any strange news stories that could be linked to his antics. After eliminating any that were explained by logic or natural occurrence, Rosie hoped they might zero in on the imp's location.

She'd been very excited about the chart when she'd made it. It was like something out of a police investigation. But now she was losing some of her enthusiasm. She wanted to be a witch, not a detective, and so far, despite her mother's promise on Christmas Day, Lydia hadn't taught her any of the Craft. Lydia claimed she had to practice on her own first, that she was too rusty to take on a pupil. How long will it take her to get in shape? Rosie wondered, growing more and more impatient.

"Here's an interesting one," Lydia said, reading a newspaper, one of many surrounding her. " 'Blizzard in Beverly Hills.' Isn't that the third freak snowstorm in California within three days?"

"Yes. I think so," Rosie replied, without much enthusiasm.

"Better put a check next to that one." There was an odd hesitation in her voice. Anyone else probably would not have noticed it. But Rosie knew her mother too well not to.

"What is it?" she asked.

"I wish I could tell you," Lydia replied, with a frown. "Look, how did the imp leave our shop?"

"Hmm." Rosie thought a minute. "Maybe he got into an empty soda bottle and we forgot and put it into the recycling bin and the truck picked him up and took him on his journey."

Lydia shook her head. "I know there's something I

should be remembering, but I'm not . . . Oh, well." She rubbed her eyes and stood up. "Time for calisthenics."

It wasn't push-ups or jumping jacks she was talking about. It was focusing energy, working on spells, gathering power—a witch's workout as it were. Turning to her daughter, Lydia said, "Would you . . ."

Rosie didn't give her a chance to finish. "Look, Mom. You said we have to catch this imp fast. You said he could be dangerous. You also said you'd let me help. Well, how am I supposed to help if you still refuse to teach me this stuff? When do I become a witch?"

Lydia picked up some newspapers and dropped them on the table. "I was just about to ask, when I was interrupted, would you care to begin your apprenticeship now?"

Rosie blinked. "Do you mean it?"

"Have you ever known me to say something I don't mean? . . . Never mind, don't answer that question." Lydia smiled.

Rosie did, too, and, scrambling to her feet, followed her mother down to the basement.

"Look at the flame," Lydia said, a short while later, as she and her daughter sat facing an orange candle in an ornate brass holder.

"Where did that candlestick come from?" Rosie asked.

"I've had it a long time," Lydia replied. "Now, forget the holder and look at the flame. . . . Let it draw all unwelcome thoughts from your mind. Breathe deeply. Concentrate on nothing but your breath and the flame. . . ."

"Why an *orange* candle? Why not white or blue—"

"Rosie!" Lydia rapped out. Then, more softly, "Rosie, no more questions. You can ask them later. The point of this exercise is for you to focus your mind and your energy. You cannot perform magic unless your entire being is focused on it."

"But . . ." But this isn't magic, Rosie wanted to say. This is staring at a candle, for God's sake. However, she held her tongue, settled down as comfortably as she could in the old metal folding chair, and gazed at the flickering light.

When Lydia at last told her the exercise was over, she wiped her watering eyes and let out a huge sigh of relief. She couldn't remember ever being so bored in her life. The five minutes she'd spent breathing and staring had been interminable. As for getting rid of unwelcome thoughts, well, the more Rosie had tried to get rid of them, the more they'd appeared. In the space of those minutes she'd wished for a bigger allowance, planned an excursion to the mall, reviewed a particularly obnoxious social studies test she'd had just before vacation, gotten hungry, and had three fantasies about Johnny Haines.

"All right," said Lydia. "Now we'll try a little scrying."

"Scrying?"

"Crystal gazing. Except we won't be using a crystal ball. That's just a nicety—and besides, it's one thing we don't have. This will work just as well, at a fraction of the cost." She pointed to an object on the table.

"But that's just a bowl of water," said Rosie.

"That's right."

"We're going to try to see the future in a bowl of water?"

"Not the future. The present—elsewhere."

Rosie looked doubtful.

"First we burn these herbs," Lydia went on, indicating the mixture in a small ashtray. She touched the candle flame to it. It flared and a wispy aromatic smoke arose.

Rosie inhaled. "Phew-whee! It smells like old blankets!"

Lydia let out a small exasperated sigh. "Rosamunde," she said, clipping off each syllable. "Do you or do you not want to be my apprentice?"

"You know I do."

"Then pay attention."

"But . . . ," Rosie began and stopped. But it *does* smell like blankets, she was going to say. Instead, lowering her eyes, she said, "Yes, ma'am," with just enough sass to make Lydia smile despite herself.

I was just like her at that age, she thought. I wanted to know and do everything all at once. And my mother wasn't any more patient with me than I am with Rosie.

In a gentler voice she said, "Okay. Let's start with something simple. Both of us will look into this bowl of water and call up a picture of the oak tree outside our house. Don't try to force the image. Just let it come."

"Okay," said Rosie, drawing her chair closer to the table and gazing into the bowl. The flame was reflected in the water. Lydia moved the candle, and the flame disappeared, leaving only dark shadows and a silvery glow.

The oak tree, Rosie said to herself. You know what it looks like. You've seen it a million times. Tall. Bare. With snow on the branches and the ragged remains of a robin's nest. You can see it now. Right here. In this bowl of water.

But all she could see were the shadows.

Oh, Lord, she complained silently. This is worse than staring at that candle. At least then I wasn't supposed to see anything but the stupid flame.

"Look at that. A whole flock of cardinals just landed in the branches. How pretty!" Lydia exclaimed.

Rosie started. Cardinals! She couldn't even see the outline of a tree and her mother saw a whole flock of birds perched in it. But she didn't want to tell Lydia that. She was afraid her mother would throw up her hands and say, "That's it. You'll never be a witch. Not now. Not ever."

"Very pretty," she lied. "Just like a photograph."

"More like a film, I'd say," said her mother.

"Oh, right. Of course. A film."

After another few excruciating minutes, Lydia told her to let go of the picture, which Rosie had no trouble doing because there was no picture to let go of.

"Now we'll try something a little harder. Who would you like to see right now if you could?"

"That's easy. Johnny Haines." Even though he hadn't returned her phone call on Christmas, she still wanted to be his girlfriend as much as ever.

"Fine. Let's call up a picture of Johnny Haines and find out what he's up to."

Rosie gulped. Oh no. Now why did I go and do that? She'll get to see him and I won't and I won't be able to fool her and pretend that I . . . "Yi yi!" Rosie gasped. There, floating in the bowl like some sort of hologram from a science-fiction movie, was Johnny Haines. He had on a hat and muffler, and he appeared to be standing somewhere, but the background was too blurry for Rosie to identify.

"He's cold," she said, watching him blow on his hands. "He's waiting for someone and he's annoyed." She saw him frown. Suddenly, another face came into view. Rosie recognized it at once. It was Betsy Brummell, Johnny's latest girl. Although she couldn't hear the words, Rosie could tell that they were having an argument.

"They'll be history next week," she said delightedly, and began to cackle.

"That's enough of that," Lydia said curtly. "Let go of that picture."

"Aw, Mom, just a little longer . . ."

"I said let go of it. Scrying is not to be confused with spying." Although she was being stern, inside Lydia felt excited. Just as she'd suspected, her daughter had a real aptitude for the art. An imaginative, bright girl like Rosie with witch's genes was almost certain to be a good scryer. It didn't matter that she had been faking it about the oak tree. She couldn't see it because it didn't interest her. It would take Rosie a while to learn that much of magic was less than interesting.

Rosie sighed. Bye-bye, Johnny. See you around—minus Betsy Brummell. Another little snicker escaped her. But she shut her eyes, and when she opened them, Johnny was gone.

"Very good," Lydia nodded. "Now, for our last image we're going to call up a picture of the imp—a wide-angle picture with sharp details that will give us clues as to where he is."

"Okay," Rosie declared. She suddenly felt assured—

even cocky. If she could call up a picture of Johnny Haines in a bowl of tap water, there was nothing she couldn't do.

"We have to concentrate hard. He may resist being seen."

"*Okay*," Rosie repeated impatiently, and she stared hard at the bowl.

Within seconds she saw him—his bushy hair, his blazing eyes. He was bouncing on a bed. With each bounce, a spring twanged out through the mattress. "Ha! There he is!" Rosie crowed.

"Yes. There he is. But where is he?" Lydia replied.

"Hmm. It looks like somebody's bedroom."

"Yes. But whose?"

"I don't know. There aren't any clues."

"There are always clues. Look, there's an aquarium and a microscope and a poster of some baseball player in a Red Sox uniform—"

"Ted Williams," Rosie interrupted. "He's an old-timer now, but still famous. I'll bet it's a kid's room."

"I'll bet you're right."

The imp jumped off the bed and disappeared from view. "Where'd he go?"

"I don't know. Quick, what else can you see in the room?" Lydia asked.

"Not much. There are some boxes in the corner and . . . Ah!" Rosie yelped.

The imp's face suddenly blotted out everything else in view. He stuck out his tongue and blew a tremendous raspberry. It was so loud Rosie had to clap her hands over her ears. "Mom, I can hear him!" she yelled.

"Oh, my God, he knows we're spying . . . uh . . .

scrying him," Lydia said. "Quick, Rosie, let go of the picture."

Rosie shut her eyes. But when she opened them, the imp was still there. He gave another deafening Bronx cheer. "I can't, Mom. I'm trying to, but I can't. Can't you do it?"

Lydia didn't answer. Rosie looked at her and, in the dim candlelight, saw beads of sweat on her mother's forehead. Oh no, she can't do it either, Rosie thought, becoming scared.

She turned back to the bowl. The imp was laughing now. He made a little gesture with his hand, and his image began to waver. Whew, he's going on his own, thought Rosie with relief.

But the relief was short lived. The water in the bowl had begun to bubble. Steam rose from the surface. The bowl itself began to clatter on the table and bounce toward her.

"Look out, Rosie! Look out!" Lydia screamed.

Rosie jumped up just in time as the glass bowl crashed to the floor, smashing into pieces and dumping boiling water inches from her feet.

For a long moment, neither Rosie nor her mother could say a word.

Then at last Lydia rose briskly. "I think that'll be all for today." She went upstairs without another word.

Rosie got a broom and dustpan, and as she began to sweep up the shards, she thought, If we ever do find the imp, I wonder just which of us is going to end up in a bottle.

Chapter Eight

On Sunday, the surfers were shivering in Malibu. In Venice on the following day, the in-line roller skaters were slipping and sliding on the icy-slick pier. Tuesday morning in Beverly Hills, shoppers on Rodeo Drive stopped asking for bathing suits and started searching for sweaters. And on Wednesday afternoon in the Hollywood hills, Danny plucked a frozen hibiscus flower and, grinning, stuck it into Laura's hair.

"It's great, isn't it?" he said, waving his arms at the snowcapped eucalyptus trees. "Isn't it great?"

"Yeah," Laura answered.

Danny turned to her. "What's the matter? You're not tired of snow already, are you? You're not feeling like Mom? 'What is it with all this snow? If I wanted snow, I could've stayed in Vermont.' " He imitated Ginny's voice quite well indeed.

Laura shook her head. "No. But I can't help wondering if maybe we're messing up the environment."

"Messing up the environment? Heck, we're probably *helping* the environment. Blowing away all the smog and stuff. And snow's good for the plants. That's what Mom always used to say back home."

"I don't know about that. These plants don't look so hot."

"Oh, come on, Laura. Who cares about a couple of plants? We're having fun, right?"

"It's more than a couple," Laura muttered.

Danny heard her and got annoyed. "Look, if you want to go home, that's fine with me. Just ask our chauffeur to take you." He turned and gestured to a car parked some ten yards away—the kind of car Adam Pauling would have called a *humdinger*. It *was* quite an outstanding car, even by L.A. standards, where outstanding cars are as common as cows in Vermont. It was a 1957 baby blue Thunderbird convertible with whitewalls, shiny chrome grillwork, and a license plate that said, HAVITALL.

Danny had taken one look at it three days before in Manny's Classic Cars' parking lot and drooled. "Dad would flip if he saw this," he said, thinking about how many times his father had taken him and Laura to the car show in Burlington. It was an excursion he'd always made time for, no matter how busy his schedule. "Man, I'd give anything to own that car."

"Oh, really? How about selling me your immortal soul?" Mr. Ed asked.

Danny's eyes narrowed. "Wait a minute. You're not . . ."

"No, I'm not. That was just a joke. However, if you truly like that car, you shall have it. After all, your wish is my command."

"But we're too young to drive," said Laura.

"Of course you are. Therefore, you need a chauffeur." Mr. Ed flicked his fingers and, presto, instead of the somewhat garish suit he'd been wearing, he was now clad in a gray uniform and cap, which he tipped.

"How are we going to get the car?" Danny asked, suddenly a bit nervous.

"Buy it, of course," answered the imp, producing a wad of bills.

Danny and Laura's eyes bugged out. "Where did that come from?" he asked.

"My pocket. Now, follow me."

And they did, hovering behind the imp and smothering giggles as he got the salesman to knock several thousand dollars off the price of the car by creating several different engine problems (all of which miraculously disappeared as soon as they drove out of the lot).

They didn't bother to find out how Mr. Ed knew about cars and how to drive them—they just took it for granted that a supernatural being could do these things.

Laura turned now to look at the car. Mr. Ed, wearing a different colored uniform today—this one a deep burgundy—was sitting behind the wheel, twitching his shoulders, bobbing his head, shaking up and down to some hot salsa music blasting out of the radio. "Wak-taka-taka. Wak-taka-taka. Chooga-chooga-looga. Wak-taka-taka. Wak-taka-taka-chooga-choo—kachunga-kay!" he sang, sounding like several percussion instruments being played simultaneously.

"Turn that down!" Laura commanded—or at least tried to. The imp's performance was too amusing, and she ended up laughing. When she turned back to Danny, he was grinning at her again.

She took the wilting flower out of her hair and stuck it behind his ear. "No, I don't want to go home. But maybe we could do something else besides making it snow."

"Sure, we can do something else," Danny replied, his grin slowly turning sly. "We can do something really American. Something that no human—or nonhuman—should miss."

"What do you mean?"

"We can take our chauffeur to a mall."

Laura was immediately both intrigued and cautious. "Well, I didn't bring much money. . . ."

"Don't worry. You won't need it," Danny dismissed.

"I guess that's true," she agreed, remembering the imp's magic pocket, thinking Danny meant the same thing.

They walked over to the car. "Hop in," he said in a sporty voice.

"Don't mind if I do," Laura answered, jumping over the door right into the seat.

Danny did the same. "The mall," he ordered. "At once."

"Sure thing, boss," the imp replied.

As Danny settled back in his seat with a smug smile, he thought, Maybe L.A. is not so bad after all.

Mr. Ed was impressed with the mall. Laura could tell by the way he kept turning his head and squawking "Creeping crawfish!" every few moments like some demented parrot.

Laura didn't blame him. The mall was sensational. Clean, climate controlled, and nearly as large as some of the Vermont towns Laura knew, it had every kind of store or stall imaginable, selling everything from pelican-shaped pool floats to cookies cut like palm trees. Today it seemed that every single one of those stalls and stores was packed with people returning too-small sweaters, ugly teapots, duplicate dish towels, and unwanted ties or searching out post-Christmas bargains for aunts and uncles and cousins they had yet to see.

A smooth voice over the PA system occasionally interrupted the holiday music to guide the shoppers from one bargain to another. "Today only, cotton candy on level one, aisle two. Buy one, get one free," the voice was saying now.

"Where should we go first?" Laura asked eagerly. "Disc Derby? Fleet Feet? The Wrap?"

"You're just dying to spend more of Mr. Ed's not-so-hard-earned money, aren't you?" Danny teased.

"And I suppose you're not," Laura huffed, rather defensively. She had been brought up not to be greedy, and she didn't like being reminded of just how quickly she'd forgotten that.

"No, I'm not, because (1) if we bring home a lot of new stuff, Mom will start asking questions."

"You didn't worry about that when we got the car."

"Oh yes, I did. I knew Mr. Ed could park it in a lot and Mom would never see it. And (2) there are more interesting things to do in this place besides shop. Right, Mr. Ed?"

They both turned to look at the imp. The imp, however, was not looking at them. The imp was gone.

"What the . . . Where did . . . ," Danny and Laura exclaimed simultaneously. The rest of their sentences were drowned out by the sharp, driving salsa music that had completely erased "Deck the Halls" over the speakers.

"There he is!" They pointed at the same time toward the middle of the aisle, where Mr. Ed, almost imperceptibly waggling his fingers and flicking his wrists, was heading away from them at a steady clip.

Danny and Laura took off. Every time they thought they'd caught up with him, Mr. Ed disappeared again. But the evidence of his handiwork was in plain sight. There was the pet shop, where all the birds were singing backup and all the fish in the big aquarium were wriggling in time to the beat. The weather store, where the salespeople and customers were huddled under umbrellas and raincoats sold there, to escape a sprinkler system gone berserk. The cotton-candy vendor and buyers swearing over newly grown beards and wigs of the sticky stuff. The popcorn machine shooting kernels high into the air nonstop and raining them down like hail. And last but not least, the Suit of Male, where all the mannequins in the window had dropped their pants and were pressing fiberglass hands to painted mouths as if to say, "Whoops."

It was at Santa's Corner that they finally found him. The elves and snow fairies were still on display, but Santa was long gone. Or at least he was supposed to be. In his place, on a throne decorated with tinsel and evergreen swags, sat the imp, dressed like old Saint Nick himself.

"Merry Christmas. Merry Christmas. Were you a good little girl? Were you a good little boy?" he demanded of the crowd beginning to form. "Come to Santa and get your Yuletide goodies." To the first girl in line he handed a two-foot-high doll that bore a remarkable resemblance to himself.

"But Christmas is over," a boy called out.

"Then get out of here, kid," Mr. Ed snapped, tossing a snowball at the boy's head.

Pulling Laura along with him, Danny pushed through the people, who complained, "Hey," "Cut it out," and "Wait your turn," until he stood squarely in front of the imp.

"Have *you* been a good little boy and a good little girl?" Mr. Ed boomed at them, whipping out a set of handcuffs and offering them to the pair.

Danny and Laura yanked him off the throne and hustled him out of the room.

"Don't you go off like that without us ever again. Got that?" Danny warned him.

Mr. Ed pulled a long, sheepish face. "I'm sorry. I'm so sorry." He shuffled and pouted like a kid about to be spanked. "It won't happen again. Honestly. Sincerely. From the bottom of my heart." He made a quick sign, and his jacket opened to reveal an anatomical drawing of a heart with an arrow pointing to the lower chambers. At the same time he clipped the handcuffs around his wrist and Danny's and gave Laura the key.

"You think this is funny? Maybe you want to go back into that cute little sack you came out of, huh?" Danny berated the imp as Laura unlocked the cuffs and slid them from his arm.

"No. No, I don't think I should like that. Not a whit," the imp said, quite seriously.

"Okay. Then you've got to remember who's the boss."

"Yes, sir."

"Who *is* the boss?"

"You are, sir, Your Highness, Your Majesty, your Imperial Fabulousness, Your Celestial Marvelocity. . . ."

"That's enough. You stay with us from now on so we can have some fun . . . and lose that Santa suit."

"Right away, boss." The imp snapped his fingers. His wardrobe went from Santa to chauffeur in what seemed the blink of an eye. But Laura could have sworn that in between she caught glimpses of a doublet, a nightgown, a tuxedo, and a gorilla costume. "Now, what do you have in mind?"

Danny paused barely a second, then said, "We'll hit the bookstore first. I want you to change all the new calendars there to last year's. Then, the shoe store, where you'll fill all the boots with Jell-O. I want the refrigerators in Fry's Appliances to burp every time somebody opens them and the computers at ElectroWorld to tell everyone, Touch Me and Die. I want the travel posters at Jaunts and Journeys to advertise special tours to Mars, Alpha Centauri, the Famous Toilets of Hollywood, the Chicken Coops of Vermont and Hell, and I want all the movies in all the octoplexes to be *Bambi Meets Godzilla*, played over and over nonstop. And that's just for starters." He looked right at the imp.

His sister, feeling suddenly left out, was speechless. When did he have time to come up with all that? she wondered.

But the imp smiled with admiration. "It's a pleasure to serve you, boss. A real pleasure." He saluted. "Now please, lead the way."

And Danny did.

Chapter Nine

"Nice underwear."

Rosie didn't exactly freeze. But she did stand perfectly still without turning around for a long moment.

She knew that voice. She knew it very well indeed. She'd been waiting for months for it to say something to her. She'd fantasized hearing it in all sorts of places—a restaurant, a dance, a park, a movie theater. But never in her wildest imagination did she think she'd hear it addressing her in Werner's lingerie department at the mall (which wasn't even a mall, just a collection of stores with thin walls between them), as she stood by the cash register with a pair of pink-flowered underpants in her hand.

Now, the old Rosie would have blushed and stammered and probably even ducked out of there as fast as possible. But this wasn't the old Rosie. Something had happened to her during the past several days—days devoted entirely to her apprenticeship. The breathing and candle-staring were actually beginning to get easier—meaning she could concentrate better on them. Lydia was so pleased with her progress, she'd taught her some simple spells and charms. "But no one becomes a witch overnight," she warned, though that was exactly what Rosie had to do. Any day now they might learn where the imp was and have to confront him. Lydia hoped Rosie wouldn't have to help with more than the basics. But she had to do her best to prepare her daughter for the worst.

"I know that," Rosie had said meekly. She did in fact feel a little humble—the scrying incident with the imp had done that to her. But she also knew she was doing very well indeed as a budding witch, and, what's more, she knew that Lydia knew.

If I can cast a spell to tell me where to find that earring I lost in May, I can turn around and look at Johnny Haines without turning colors.

Taking a deep breath, she pivoted gracefully and smiled. "Hello, Johnny. Fancy meeting you here."

Johnny Haines smiled back. If teeth could be said to flirt, then Johnny's teeth were top-notch at it. Likewise his dancing blue eyes, shiny auburn hair, and even the smattering of freckles across his adorably oversized nose. "I'm exchanging Mom's Christmas present." With a complete lack of embarrassment, he held up a flannel nightgown. "I got her the wrong size. She was too busy to come here herself, so I said I'd take care of it."

"That's nice of you," Rosie responded, amazed that she wasn't babbling at him.

"What can I say? I'm a nice guy." He shrugged. Then

he asked, "So, what are you doing your English report on?"

"This great book by Shirley Jackson called *We Have Always Lived in a Castle*. The main character is this weird eighteen-year-old girl who lives with her sister. She poisoned all the rest of her family because she hated them. It's very well written."

"Well written, huh?" Johnny's mouth quirked in a grin.

Rosie got embarrassed. She didn't know why she should be, but she was. "What are you writing yours on?"

"I don't know yet."

"But it's due next Friday."

"Yeah, well . . ." He shrugged again. "It'll get done. Somehow."

The cashier rang up Rosie's order, leaving her with a choice. She could say, "Bye, Johnny. See you in school next week," or she could try to continue this conversation with the boy of her dreams and see just where it went. She chose the latter.

"How's your vacation been?" she asked, taking her bag from the counter. "Did you get the new racing skates you wanted?"

Johnny handed the new and old nightgowns to the cashier for exchange and said with surprise, "Yeah, I did. How'd you know I wanted racing skates?"

"Oh . . . I heard you talking to some of the other kids about them. Are you good at racing?"

"Yeah, I'm pretty good."

"Well, then maybe you'll make the Olympic team."

"I'm not that good."

"Oh, don't say that," Rosie urged somewhat intensely, staring into his eyes. "You can do anything you want, if you want it hard enough."

"Yeah?" Johnny looked back at her. "You really believe that?"

"Absolutely."

"So, what do you want hard enough, Rosie Rivera?" he asked, teeth, eyes, hair all doing their flirty dance.

To be a great witch. To catch a crazy imp. To go out with you tonight, New Year's Eve, Rosie thought, but didn't dare say any of it.

"Here you are, young man," said the cashier. Rosie thought her timing was rather good.

Johnny turned and took the package and receipt. When he faced Rosie again, he seemed to have forgotten the question. "Well, I've got to go. I told Jason I'd help him. There's a party at his place tonight. His parents promised to stay out of our way."

"Oh, that's nice." Rosie was suddenly disappointed. So Johnny Haines had talked to her. So what? He was going to some party tonight while she and Lydia practiced, practiced, practiced, then, exhausted, probably fell asleep before the clock struck midnight. "Are you taking Betsy Brummell?" she asked, rather meanly.

"No, I broke up with her. Her idea of a date is trying on clothes while I hang around waiting for her."

Rosie laughed, then, feeling guilty, said, "She *is* a very good dresser."

"Yeah, well, good dressing isn't everything."

Was it her imagination, or was he examining her old

faded red sweater and too-new blue jeans, Rosie wondered, feeling her confidence slipping away again.

Then Johnny said, "What are you doing tonight?"

"Uh, nothing much."

"Why don't you come to Jason's party? It starts at eight. A lot of the kids from our class will be there."

"I . . . I . . . ," Rosie began to stammer. Get it together, *witch*, she told herself. "I'd love to go."

"Good. You know where Jason lives, don't you? Twenty-two Redfern—the big gray house."

"Right."

"See you there later, okay?"

"Okay."

He winked and, package under his arm, sauntered away.

Rosie gazed after him, heart clanking like the old water heater in her basement. A date, she thought. I have a date with Johnny Haines. Almost.

"It's almost midnight!" someone called.

All the bobbing bodies stopped and straightened their silly paper hats and clutched their noisemakers. Rosie's hat was a bright, sparkling red, and she intended to keep it forever. Johnny Haines had selected it for her. He'd come right up to her at the table and picked it out of the selection there. "A rose has to wear red," he'd said as he put it on her head.

Then all night long he'd stuck nearby—or, at least, so it seemed to Rosie. Even when he was dancing or talking with someone else, she would glance over and see him looking back. It made her smile a little broader, her posture a little straighter, and her cheeks a lot more glowing.

But oddly enough, at that moment Rosie was not thinking of Johnny Haines. She was thinking about Lydia. It was the very first New Year's Eve Rosie was spending away from her mother, and she suddenly felt a little bit guilty about it. Here she was, having a good time at a good party, while Lydia sat home alone, practicing and probably worrying about the imp.

She had been very preoccupied when Rosie was getting ready for the party. It had taken her three attempts to tie the bow in her daughter's long hair, a task that her nimble fingers would have normally accomplished in one. And she kept muttering to herself, "It's right there, on the tip of my memory, the edge of my tongue. . . ." Even if Rosie had been in a reassuring mood, she wouldn't have known just then how to help out her mother.

Now she found herself wishing that Lydia had a boyfriend. *It's been a long time since she went out on a date. She should be more sociable. This isn't the Middle Ages. A witch doesn't have to hide away in some hovel in the woods. I certainly won't,* Rosie thought.

"Ten, nine, eight . . . ," several voices began to count.

Rosie looked up. Johnny Haines was right beside her, grinning. "Come on, Rivera. You're a brain. You can count backward from ten to one."

Rosie grinned back and joined in. "Four, three, two, one . . . Happy New Year!"

Everyone began to hug and kiss. So it was perfectly natural for Johnny and Rosie to do the same. But Rosie couldn't help noticing that Johnny's kiss seemed a little more than just friendly.

"Happy New Year, Rosie Rivera," he breathed into her ear. "I'll call you tomorrow."

"Oh," said Rosie. "Oh, my." It probably wasn't what a witch would say, but it was the best she could come up with.

The party went on a little while longer. Rosie floated through it, then floated all the way home.

When she got there, all the lights were on. "Mom?" she called, opening the door. "Mom, you'll never guess what happened. Mom, where are you?"

She checked all over the house, including the basement, but didn't find Lydia. Could she be in the shop at this hour? Opening the door that led to it, she yelled, "Mom, are you there?"

There was no answer. Too exhilarated from the past few hours' events to be fearful, she walked right into the back room, which was used as an office. There were piles of papers on the desk, all neatly arranged. Receipts, it looked like, but no Lydia.

"Mom?"

Suddenly Lydia popped up from under the desk, where she'd been scrambling on the floor. Rosie yelped. Lydia didn't notice. She was staring at a receipt clutched in her hand. "This is it," she read. "This has got to be it."

"What's got to be it, Mom?" Rosie asked, bewildered.

"Thank heavens he wrote down his number. I've got to call him right now. It's late, but this can't wait."

"*What's* got to be it, Mom? Who do you have to call?"

At last, Lydia looked up. "Oh, Rosie. You're home. Did you have a good time?"

"It was great, and will you please tell me what's going on here?"

"Ah." Lydia's eyes were bright. The tension and frustration Rosie had seen on her mother's face recently were gone—replaced, at least for now, with an expression of triumph. "I remembered at last. There was a customer here in the shop with the imp."

"That's right. I heard the bell ring. But I didn't know whether or not the imp let the person in," said Rosie.

"He let him in, all right. He *waited* on him. The man bought a bunch of tricks and took them away with him. One of the tricks was Winter Magic. I noticed it was open and I tied up the cords. How was I supposed to know our *Impus mischievous* was in the sack?"

"Oh no! So that's how he got out of the shop! Who was the customer? Is that his receipt?" Picking up her mother's fervor, Rosie leaned over her shoulder. "Adam Pauling. Twenty-five fifty-one Blue Spruce Road, Pendelton, Vermont, 555-7692. That's not too far from here."

"I've got to call him now," Lydia reiterated. She reached for the phone and dialed the number. "Damn," she said, surprising Rosie because she never swore. "It's his answering machine."

"Well, Mom, it *is* New Year's Eve," Rosie reminded her.

Lydia flapped a hand at her daughter, meaning be quiet, took a deep breath, and smoothly, urgently, said, "This is Lydia Rivera of Quicker than the Eye, the magic shop where you recently purchased some items. It is imperative that you phone me at once concerning the destination of these items. It may be vital to the health and safety of you or your loved ones." She left her number and hung up. "There." She turned to her daughter. "We'll get that imp, Rosie. Sooner or later, we'll get him."

"I hope it's sooner, Mom," declared Rosie.

"So do I," Lydia replied. "So do I."

Chapter Ten

Just past midnight, while Rosie Rivera was still at the party dancing with Johnny Haines to "Auld Lang Syne," forty-five miles away Adam Pauling rose from his sofa and reached for the phone.

It had been one of those increasingly infrequent nights when Adam was actually at home rather than in a motel. And all evening long he'd been feeling as lost and out of place there as a bumblebee in a broom closet. He'd known for some time that he ought to sell the house. But he kept hoping that, despite their divorce, Ginny might want to get back together and maybe live there again with the kids. He had never actually suggested this to her. He kept trying to find the right time.

Well, now it's a new year. What time could be better, he thought, punching in her number.

The phone rang six times. With each ring, Adam's excitement and resolve faded a little. Then at last, on the seventh ring, someone answered, "Hello, hello, hello. Brawling residence."

"What? Danny is that you?"

"Not last time I looked."

Adam frowned. "Is this 555–1844?"

"Maybe. Hum a few bars and I'll tell you if it is."

Suddenly there were some scuffling noises and a muffled voice saying, "Give me that. I told you not to answer the phone." Then a third voice got on. "Hello. Pauling residence," it said.

"Ginny! Happy New Year!" Adam exclaimed, relieved.

"It's Laura, Dad."

"Oh, Laura. Jeez, you're sounding more and more like your mother every day. . . . Well, Happy New Year to *you*."

"Thanks, Dad. But we've got three more hours to go here before midnight."

"Oh yes. That's right. I forgot about the time difference. . . . So, how are you celebrating this New Year's Eve? Do you and Danny have exciting plans?"

Laura hesitated. "No. Not really. We're just hanging out with our . . . neighbor." Adam wondered if he'd imagined the slight squeak and breathlessness in her tone, as if she were not quite telling the truth.

"Was that who answered the phone?"

"Yes. That's him. He likes to . . . um . . . joke around."

"And your mom? How about her plans?"

"She just went out."

"On a date?"

Laura paused again. "Yeah," she said at last. "With Biff." The disapproval in her voice was clear.

"Oh, well. No reason why she shouldn't be enjoying herself tonight," Adam replied, slightly uncertain as to whether or not he was trying to reassure his daughter or himself. "People like to celebrate on New Year's Eve. . . . Go out on a date, for a change."

"She's gone out on dates before, Dad. And with Biff."

"Oh."

Then, confidentially, Laura lowered her voice. "But I don't think he'll be around a lot longer, Dad. . . . Ow! Danny!"

"What was that?"

"Nothing."

"Why won't this Biff be around much longer?"

"Oh, her boyfriends never are."

Adam digested that in silence. Then he said, "Well, tell her . . . tell her Happy New Year for me, will you, Laura?"

"Sure, Dad."

"Great! You and your brother have a nice night, now. Don't drink too much champagne." He laughed heartily at his feeble joke.

"You don't have to worry about that, Dad," Laura replied.

They bade each other good-night and hung up.

Adam stared down at the receiver and let out a very long sigh. He stood up, sat back down on the sofa, turned on the TV, and turned it off again. He went into the kitchen, ate half a donut and threw the rest away. "I can't stay here. Not tonight," he said aloud, as if apologizing to the house. Then he got into his coat and his car. Talking to his sheepskin-covered steering wheel as if it were a pet, he drove until it was twelve o'clock in L.A. Then he checked into the first motel he found.

As he lay in the cool, clean, anonymous bed, he wondered why the strange voice that had answered his family's phone was so oddly familiar. He was still wondering when he fell asleep.

"You almost gave it away," Danny accused.

"You almost gave it away," the imp mimicked.

"I did not," Laura defended herself. "And you didn't have to poke me."

"I did not. And you didn't have to poke me," aped Mr. Ed.

"Shut up!" Danny and Laura yelled at him.

He pursed his lips and contritely blinked his eyes.

Laura toyed with the phone cord. "I wonder why he called," she said.

"Who, Dad? Wasn't it to wish Mom a Happy New Year?"

"Well, yeah, but . . . I think he misses her, us."

"Maybe."

"Do you think maybe she misses him, too?"

"She doesn't act like she does. All those dates."

"Ates . . . ates . . . ates," Mr. Ed echoed.

"Yeah, but maybe she goes out a lot because she misses

Dad. You know, to forget about how much she does."

"Uz . . . uz . . . uz."

"Laura the shrink," Danny scoffed.

"Ink . . . ink . . . ink," the imp reverberated.

"Shut up!" yelled Danny and Laura.

Mr. Ed made a zipping motion at his mouth and an actual zipper appeared.

"Weird!" Laura exclaimed.

Danny looked at the kitchen clock. "We'd better get going. They should be there by now. We want our timing to be right."

"You really think this will work?" asked Laura, sounding as though she almost wished he would say it wouldn't and call the whole thing off.

Danny didn't oblige. "Oh, it'll work all right, won't it, Mr. Ed?" he said fiercely.

The imp pointed to the zipper and made a helpless gesture.

Danny sighed impatiently. "You can talk now."

Mr. Ed snapped his fingers. The zipper disappeared. "Thanks, boss," he said. "Now, what was your question?"

"Forget it," Danny snapped. "Just go get the car."

"In a hurry, eh, boss?" the imp asked with a leer. Without waiting for an answer, he gleefully scampered out the door.

Lunacy, said the sign in white-gold neon script.

"Is this it?" said Danny. "It doesn't look like any restaurant I'd want to go to."

"I saw an ad for this place," Laura mused, taking in the

sweeping driveway, the sculpted trees and bushes festooned with elegant twinkling lights, the picture windows that let you look straight through the building to the patio beyond. "It showed this man and this woman all dressed up. They were dancing. She was bent all the way backward and he was holding her with one arm. Underneath them it said, 'Go Mad in the Moonlight.' "

"The moonlight? You mean they eat outside here?"

"Yes. Mom said they call it *alfresco*. It's supposed to be more romantic that way."

"Not when we're finished it won't be. . . . Outside's good, though. If those bushes go all the way around, we can hide behind them. Then we'll be able to see them, but they won't be able to see us."

"Let's find out," said Laura. "Drive around the block, Mr. Ed."

Behind the restaurant, it turned out, was a parking lot, banded by bushes. Mr. Ed didn't park there, though. Instead, he chose a quiet side street. Then, he, Danny, and Laura walked to the restaurant's parking lot and huddled in the shrubbery.

"I see them," Laura hissed.

Danny scanned the patio. There they were, dancing, his mother and Biff. A slow dance. Danny had seen his parents dance a few times. His father was fabulous. He made his mother look fabulous, too. Biff, on the other hand, was barely adequate. Mostly he just held Ginny tight and swayed back and forth in place. Ginny, however, did not seem to mind. She was smiling, leaning against Biff, with her eyes closed.

80

Danny's stomach felt as though he'd eaten a very sour apple.

The song ended, and Biff and Ginny walked back to their table. Laura noticed that he pulled out the chair for her mother and that he filled her champagne glass from a bottle chilling in an ice bucket. Only then did Biff begin to nibble, with his mouth neatly closed, on a dinner roll. "He has good manners," Laura whispered. "Mom's a real sucker for that."

"Did you hear that, Mr. Ed?" Danny rasped. "Our mother goes for etiquette. What a shame she's about to be so disappointed in her date."

"A terrible shame," the imp agreed. He made several passes with his fingers and grunted three times like a pig. Then he stood still and watched.

Danny and Laura watched, too. For several minutes it seemed as though nothing was happening. Biff and Ginny laughed and chatted. A waiter arrived with their dinner. The brook trout and lobster looked marvelous, and Laura's stomach grumbled.

"Shh," Danny hushed, as if she'd done it on purpose.

"I didn't . . . ," Laura began to protest.

But her brother didn't even hear her. "Look!" He poked her.

She looked. Biff was still chatting and laughing, but at the same time he was pulling off bits of his roll, balling them up, and pitching them at Ginny.

At first Ginny smiled. She must think it's some kind of joke, Laura thought. But then she saw her mother grow irritated. She could read her lips saying, "Stop it! Cut it out!"

Abruptly Biff did.

"What did you do that for?" Ginny gestured.

Biff's expression was blankly innocent. He picked up his water glass and began to blow bubbles into it. Then he smiled engagingly at her and very genteelly took a sip of water.

Ginny stared at him, then began to eat her dinner in wary silence.

Biff said something, and she smiled slightly. He said something else, and she laughed. Still smiling, she picked up her nutcracker and focused on opening the lobster claw. When she glanced up, her smile disappeared.

Biff was holding the trout in his hands, swimming it up and down the table, making it ride imaginary rapids and leap over invisible cascades. "Glub glub," he said.

Ginny's face flicked from one expression to another, all of them variations on shock, perplexity, and disgust.

Biff was oblivious. When he finished playing with the fish, he stuck the whole thing in his mouth. Like a cartoon cat, he extracted only the bony skeleton.

"Eww," said Laura. "That's gross. Does he have to be so gross?"

But Danny was biting his knuckles to keep from laughing.

Ginny stood up.

Biff stood up, too.

All of a sudden the band, which had been playing a waltz, broke into a loud rendition of an old rock song called "You Can't Sit Down."

Before she could get away, Biff pulled Ginny out onto the dance floor and proceeded to put on a show that would have had Fred Astaire, Michael Jackson, and Paula Abdul agog. He whirled, kicked, did splits, dives, and bends that were clearly impossible for any normal human being to do. The other dancers and diners stared and buzzed. Ginny stood there, frozen, hands pressed to her cheeks in horror.

Danny no longer bothered to bite his knuckles. He was doubled over in hysterics. "Go . . . mad . . . in the . . . moonlight," he gasped between giggles. Mr. Ed watched him with great satisfaction.

Laura, however, was disturbed by the look on her mother's face—and then, even more so, when the music and murmuring suddenly stopped and Biff lay on the floor, clutching his spine and groaning.

Mr. Ed sprawled out at Danny and Laura's feet and mimicked him.

Danny roared.

"This isn't funny!" yelled Laura, forgetting that she was supposed to be hiding. "We can't leave him there like that. . . ."

Danny kept laughing.

"I mean it, Danny." She turned to the imp. "Fix him up. Now!"

Mr. Ed turned to Danny. "What do you think, boss? Should I do what she says?"

"Gee . . . I don't know . . . I'd kind of like to see more of his performance. . . ."

"Danny!"

He frowned. Why was Laura so upset? The guy was probably faking. But just in case he wasn't . . . "All right, all right," Danny said. "Can't you take a joke? Fix him up, Mr. Ed."

The imp waggled his fingers, and immediately Biff sprang to his feet, gingerly feeling his sacroiliac. "Hey, it's okay. I'm okay. In fact I'm wonderful. I'm terrific. I'm sensational. This is the happiest night of my life," he loudly proclaimed. "A toast! We must have a toast to me and my stunning honey bun, Virginia." He grabbed a bottle of champagne from a waiter's tray and poured it over Ginny's head. She screeched.

"Hey!" Danny barked. "That wasn't necessary."

"Sorry, boss. I got carried away," the imp replied.

Laura looked sharply at him. He grinned at her. It made the hairs on her neck stand up.

"You . . . you lunatic!" they heard Ginny yelling, wiping at her face and hair with napkins someone had handed her, trying to protect her silk dress from ruin. Turning on her heel, she ran off to the ladies' room.

Danny, Laura, and Mr. Ed watched her go. "Nice job," Danny said, "except for the champagne shower."

"Thanks, boss," said the imp.

They hurried to their car and slid inside. Mr. Ed drove off.

"Well, scratch that guy off the list," Danny said enthusiastically to his sister.

"Yeah," Laura replied flatly.

"We won't be seeing him around again."

"Right."

"Hey, what's bugging you?" Danny asked impatiently. "The guy's fine. We fixed him up like you wanted us to."

When Laura didn't say anything, he went on. "And you wanted Mom to dump him just as much as I did."

Laura was still quiet. How could she tell him what was bothering her? What *was* bothering her? That he'd laughed when Biff hurt his back? No, Danny probably didn't even think he was really hurt. That Mr. Ed listened to Danny and not her? Maybe. But was he even listening to Danny? What if Danny only thinks he can control Mr. Ed? What if Mr. Ed is controlling him? The thought gave her the shivers.

"I'm . . . I'm worried about things getting out of hand," she said aloud.

"Don't be ridiculous. Everything's totally under control. Right, Mr. Ed?"

"You said it, boss," the imp said.

Laura looked at him. In the rearview mirror she could see his face. His nose had grown a foot long, like Pinocchio's. Laura blinked. When she looked again, it was back to its regular shape.

"See," Danny said. "There's nothing to worry about. Nothing at all."

"Right," said Laura, pulling her jacket tight against a sudden wave of cold she felt right down to her bones.

Chapter Eleven

So, if a diamond is the hardest mineral, what can you use to cut one, Rosie?" asked Mr. Catalan, the lanky ninth-grade science teacher.

"Another diamond," Rosie replied, barely a beat too slow.

"Very good—and here I thought you were daydreaming." Mr. Catalan shook his head in wonder at his own stupidity.

Rosie gave a condescending smile as if agreeing with his estimate of himself. The class sniggered conspiratorially. She ignored them. She wasn't interested in making a big deal out of this. She just wanted to put Mr. Catalan in his place so he would leave her alone to go on daydreaming, which she most certainly *had* been doing all through his boring class.

Rosie had a lot to daydream about. For once, instead of inventing fantasies about Johnny Haines, Rosie was replaying the actual events of the past two days. Not only had she and Johnny spent New Year's Eve together but also New Year's Day.

He had called as he'd promised he would and invited her to go skating. He was, of course, a fabulous skater. Rosie wasn't bad—and Johnny made her look even better. They'd flown around and around the pond, a laughing blur of red and blue, until their frozen noses told them it was time to stop and have some of the hot cider Lydia had suggested Rosie bring along in her thermos. Then he'd given her an absolutely divine kiss. Rosie couldn't remember having had a more perfect date. Actually, Rosie couldn't remember having had any date, except in her imagination—and her imagination had never come up with anything finer. She gave a delicious little shiver.

"Psst," a voice called. It was Choogie Marshak, at the desk across from hers. Choogie, who was sure to be the students' choice for Most Preppy come graduation day, held up her notebook. "Saw you with the Jack of Hearts yesterday. Lucky dog!" she'd written.

Even though Choogie could hardly be labeled a friend, Rosie couldn't resist writing back to her, "I'm going out with him tonight, too."

Choogie fluttered a hand over her heart, as if to show how it was beating.

"If this mineral—pyrite—can be scratched by quartz, but not by orthoclase feldspar, what would be its hardness, Choogie?"

Choogie's hand paused in midflutter. "Uh . . ."

"6 ½," wrote Rosie on the edge of her notebook.

"6 ½," said Choogie.

"Well. It's nice to see the class so wide awake," said Mr. Catalan, turning to the board.

"Thanks," Choogie mouthed. Rosie returned with a think-nothing-of-it shrug. Choogie was a useful ally to have. By noon, word of Rosie's good deed and good luck with Johnny Haines would be all over the school, and that suited Rosie just fine. She wanted everyone to know that Johnny was hers. With luck—and skill—she intended to keep him that way.

She planned to cast a hands-off spell that would ensure that no other girl could snare him. She wouldn't tell Lydia about it, though. It had been hard enough to get Lydia to cast a prosperity spell last week, and she had only agreed to do it because finding the imp might require money.

But as for other spells, Lydia didn't believe in practicing any of them except for those needed to capture the imp or the basic ones given to Rosie as "homework." She'd hammered away at a summoning spell—the most difficult and desperate of all measures they might need to use on the creature—which Rosie kept screwing up, confusing the words *good* and *will* and *strength* because her mind kept drifting away to her new boyfriend. But Lydia wouldn't sanction one extra little hands-off spell. She'd dismiss it as inappropriate or unworthy of the Craft, even though Rosie was certain it would only help her concentrate on her studies by giving her peace of mind about the very distracting Johnny Haines. However, Rosie had learned that it was useless to argue with her—and, now that she had the proper training, useful to do things on the sly.

The bell rang then. In the past, Rosie would have melted into the crowd, willing herself to be as inconspicuous as possible. But now she took her time, sashaying out of the classroom and into the hallway, where Johnny was waiting to walk her to their next class.

Five girls said hello to him on the way. He greeted each and every one warmly. A hands-off spell, definitely. And soon, thought Rosie, who herself was receiving interested looks from several boys who'd never noticed her before.

As they approached their English class, Johnny brought up the book report that was due at the end of the week. He surprised Rosie by mentioning that he'd started reading *The Changeover* by Margaret Mahy, a book she'd recommended. She felt very flattered that he'd remembered it and also taken her taste so seriously.

"I got it out of the library last period. Ms. Cotter raved about it, too. I just hope I can finish it on time for the paper," he said, not looking particularly worried about it. He paused, as if coming up with a new idea. "Hey, in case I don't, do you think maybe you can help me along? You know the book so well."

"Sure," Rosie agreed, pleased that he'd asked.

"Maybe we can work on it tomorrow night."

Tomorrow night! Rosie nearly gasped. Their fourth date in a row, if you counted Jason's party, which she most definitely did. "Of course," she was about to say, when she suddenly flashed on her mother's face. "We have to work. We have to practice. We have to catch that imp," she could hear her say, and she felt her guilt rise like the steam from one of Lydia's herbal concoctions.

"Uh . . . uh . . . ," she stammered and was still hemming and hawing when Susanna Turnbull, the prettiest girl in their class, sauntered up to them.

"Just who I was looking for," said Susanna, smiling at Johnny. "I have to do a portrait for my art class and I thought you'd be a great subject. How about coming over to my house tomorrow night after dinner?"

He turned to Rosie, and his blue eyes made her forget all about Lydia, all about practicing, all about the imp.

In a clear, ringing voice, she told him, "I'd love to help you out tomorrow night, Johnny."

He grinned at her. Then he said to Susanna, "Thanks for the invite, but no can do. I'll be busy then."

Yeah, thought Rosie, smiling brazenly at a stunned and staring Susanna Turnbull. Real busy. Tomorrow night and every night, if I have anything to say about it.

Chapter Twelve

Green. All together now, say, 'Greeeeennnn.' "

"Greeeeennnn," repeated the seventh-grade class, giggling along with Ms. Osier, who was costumed as a leafy plant. They were dying to know what their well-liked science teacher would come up with next.

Danny did not join in. Nor did he care what his teacher had planned. He was too busy thinking about his own plans. In a few days, he, Laura, and Mr. Ed were going to Cosmopolitan Studios to see a TV show being taped, and Danny was pondering what havoc he wanted Mr. Ed to wreak there.

Maybe I'll have him change the colors of all the lights to something weird or have the microphones make rude noises, he thought. How about some stinky smells, too— after all, the show is about guys who work in a sewer.

". . . in here for five days with water, but no light. I'm dying, dying, dying . . . ," came Ms. Osier's muffled voice from the closet.

The class was rapt. Danny yawned. I'll give her the note tomorrow, he said to himself. He had Ms. Osier for homeroom as well as for science, so permission slips went to her. He'd decided to get Mr. Ed to forge two notes, one for each of them, so they wouldn't be missed when they cut school. Laura was upset by the idea of forgery, especially since it had to do with school. Laura cared too much about things like school, he told himself, whereas he didn't. Especially since Mr. Ed had appeared. After all, what was school compared to the great high jinks they pulled off with him? What use is an education when it can't give you the power you get from a tame genie?

But Laura doesn't see it that way, Danny thought. In fact, she doesn't even think going to the TV studio is such a hot idea. Ever since New Year's Eve, she's been weird. She's getting as bad as Mom.

"Ah, oh. Light! Light! I'm going to live after all!" Ms. Osier shouted as Barney Bamboski opened the closet door on cue. "Thank you! Thank you!" She danced over to the window and lifted her arms to the sunlight. The class cheered.

Danny frowned. He was thinking about his mother. She'd also gone strange since New Year's Eve. On New Year's Day, muttering things under her breath, such as "A woman needs a man like a fish needs a bicycle," she'd cleaned the house from top to bottom, causing Danny a jolt of concern, since he wasn't exactly sure where Mr.

Ed was hiding. But then, the imp could take care of himself, he figured.

Ginny had also refused to answer any phone calls and announced abruptly that she was going to send Danny to charm school so there'd at least be one polite man in the world.

It didn't take a major brain to realize she was upset about Biff.

She's better off without that jerk, Danny thought, even if she doesn't realize it yet. In the meantime, I'll get Mr. Ed to do something nice for her. Like fill all the vases in the house with flowers. Yellow roses. That's what Dad always used to bring her when he came back from one of his long trips. I'll tell Mr. Ed to do that today.

"Okay. So why do I need light?" Ms. Osier asked the class.

"To make food," they called back.

"Right. You probably learned that answer in second grade. But now we're going to look at that food-making process in more detail. Think greeeeennnn."

"Greeeeennnn," came the response.

Danny's desk vibrated with the hum. He absentmindedly laid his hands on it. I wonder what Mr. Ed is doing now? he thought. He felt a twinge of concern. He wouldn't get into trouble, would he? No, he promised to behave. And he will. He knows who's boss.

Smiling to himself, he turned toward the window and nearly jumped out of his seat. There, grinning and duckwalking along the ledge, was none other than the imp.

What the heck are you doing here? Danny signaled. Go home!

The imp began to play air guitar in a perfect impersonation of Chuck Berry.

Get out of here, Danny mouthed, yanking his thumb at him.

"Danny, what's going on?" Ms. Osier was staring at him.

With a start, he whipped his head around. "Nothing, Ms. Osier," he said, trying to make his voice as neutral as possible. Just my luck that she's always watching me, he thought, and all because she caught me reading *Snowmobile* magazine last month and doing those cartoons of her a few weeks ago.

The teacher glanced at the window. Involuntarily, Danny did, too. There was nothing there now, except the empty paper cup that had been sitting there all day. Where did he go? Danny wondered. He suddenly felt uncomfortably warm.

After a pause, Ms. Osier turned to the board. "The name of this process, as most of you probably remember, is . . ." She scrawled the word across it. *"Photosynthesis.* Let's give it a cheer. Photo-syn-thesis." She pranced around like a cheerleader, ending in a big leap.

The class mimicked her.

"Louder!" she commanded. "Photo-syn-thesis!"

"Photo-syn-thesis!" bellowed the students.

"Once more! Photo-syn-whoops!" Ms. Osier froze as the leaves of her costume suddenly drooped and withered.

The kids giggled, thinking it was part of her performance. Then all at once five of them on the left side of the room screamed. Danny stared at them. They were wrapped all around with the bean vines the class had been growing. Their screams had hardly died down when the kids sitting by the right wall began to shriek as the supply closet opened, raining bags of peat pots and potting soil on their heads. The cries were echoed by the boys and girls at the back of the classroom, who were being watered by a short but effective hose attached to the sink.

Danny whirled toward the window. There, once again, was Mr. Ed, fingers twitching. Danny stared angrily at him. How dare he do this without my instructions?

The imp cocked his head and winked outrageously, and Danny suddenly wanted to laugh. Maybe he's doing this to please me, he thought, looking around the chaotic room. It *was* pretty funny—prissy Belinda Cheney, all covered with dirt; big bully Rob Dibble panicking at a plant; smelly Freddy Fletters, who took a bath maybe once a month, nicely soaked. Then Danny did laugh.

But he pulled himself together quickly and, looking back at Mr. Ed, made a cutting motion at his throat.

The imp didn't knock it off at once, though. He let the vines keep entangling, the supplies keep falling, the hose keep squirting his victims.

Danny gestured again and again until at last Mr. Ed waved his hands and stopped the action. Then, with a deep bow and some self-applause, he took off.

Ms. Osier stood up, surveying the mess. At her seat, Belinda was crying. Several other kids were, too. A lot more were laughing and asking their teacher how she'd done that.

Danny watched her being torn between scaring them

by admitting she'd had nothing to do with it and trying to settle everyone down. And the hot uncomfortable feeling returned. I'd better not tell Laura about this, he thought.

He volunteered to get a mop and a bucket and was glad when Ms. Osier agreed to let him leave the room.

Chapter Thirteen

"Whew," said Lydia. "What a day! I counted at least forty customers!" She was closing out the register. The take had tripled since she'd cast the prosperity spell. It was as if every kid—and even some grown-ups—who'd gotten money for the holidays had suddenly decided to spend it in her shop.

"Oh, what a little magic can do," sang Rosie.

"Magic is working with the patterns that already exist in the universe. The energy was right for our business to increase; we just helped stream that energy along the right path."

"Whatever you say, Mom," Rosie smirked. She was amused at what she considered her mother's rationalizations. Amused, but also bothered. After all, what was so bad about using a trick or two to improve your life? Nothing, as far as Rosie was concerned. But Lydia still seemed a little embarrassed that she had had to resort to magic to make the business work.

Ignoring her daughter's teasing, Lydia counted out the cash, noted the amount in the ledger, and stowed the money in the safe. Then she picked up the phone, dialed Adam Pauling's number, and left her fourth message on his answering machine. Why doesn't the man call me back? she wondered. Is he out of town? But surely he'd call in for his messages, wouldn't he? She was feeling worried again. Too much time was passing, and they hadn't gotten nearer to catching the imp. She felt in her bones that every day, every hour he was loose was a moment closer to catastrophe.

"Well," she said aloud, giving herself a mental shake. "It's time to practice the protection spell. We've got to make sure when we meet up with the imp that he can't harm us."

"Now?" Rosie asked.

"Yes, of course, now. You have a better time?"

Rosie hesitated. She was going over to Johnny Haines's house in an hour and a half. His parents were out for the evening, and they were going to order pizza to eat while she helped write his English paper. They hadn't gotten around to it the night before. Although Lydia did not disapprove of her dating, she had grown increasingly annoyed at the time it was taking away from Rosie's witchcraft studies.

Rosie felt she was doing well enough in her studies. After all, she'd already won the Jack of Hearts, hadn't she?

Just yesterday he'd told her she was the most fascinating girl he'd ever met. "That's right. I am," she'd replied boldly, making him laugh.

Furthermore, despite her mother's sense of urgency, she was becoming convinced that perhaps it didn't matter so much after all whether they captured the imp. He's obviously not going to bother us anymore. Maybe he's not really bothering anyone. But she didn't say that to Lydia. One look at her mother's face made her reply, "No. I can practice now—for a while."

"I made us each an amulet," Lydia said when they went down to the basement. From a wooden box on the table she produced two small red silk bags tied with silver cord. "They're filled with protective herbs—rosemary, sage, poppy seed, and orrisroot," Lydia explained. "The moon symbol is also a strong charm against nasty spirits." She pointed to a delicately embroidered silver crescent. "It must always be shown with the horns pointing left, the way they do when the moon is waxing. Otherwise it won't work."

"That's beautiful," Rosie said, impressed with her mother's handiwork. "I didn't know you could sew like that."

"I can when I have to. It's a skill you ought to learn."

"I don't have time," Rosie muttered.

Lydia let it pass. "Now, just wearing the amulet will help some, but not enough. What we both need to practice most is the Silver Spiral. It's a kind of force field, invisible to everyone except the person using it."

"How do we use it?"

"We have to concentrate on the silver cord until we see it not as a cord but a band of light. Then you and I each take the light and make separate spirals of it around our bodies. Eventually you won't have to look at the cord to start the spiral. You'll be able to summon it up at will."

"No problem," Rosie said arrogantly.

Lydia bit back a response.

They both settled down to concentrate on the cord.

Rosie was able to see it as a band of light very soon indeed. And by the time Lydia told her to turn it into a spiral, she'd already been encircling herself with it for several minutes.

"Can I turn it off now?" she asked impatiently a few minutes after that.

Again Lydia held her tongue. "All right. We'll rest and then see if you can bring back the spiral without looking at the cord."

During the break, Rosie fidgeted in her seat. We must have been at this for half an hour, forty-five minutes. It's definitely past six o'clock. I heard the clock chime a while ago. I need at least half an hour to get ready for my date with Johnny. I hope Lydia doesn't think I'm going to work on this all night.

"All right," said Lydia at last. "Now let's see if you can call up the spiral without—"

"There. I've already done it," Rosie interrupted. "Can we continue this later?" A lot later, she added silently.

From upstairs they heard the clock faintly ring once. "Six-thirty," said Lydia. "I suppose we can pause for the news. See if there are any new leads we can follow up while we're waiting to hear from Mr. Pauling."

"Actually, Lydia, I don't really have time to watch the news right now. I'm going over to Johnny's. Anyway, we're taping the show like we always do, in case there's something worth reviewing, which there hasn't been all week." Rosie stood up.

Lydia did, too. As her daughter moved toward the stairs, Lydia reached out, grabbed her, and, with no apparent effort at all, nearly flung her back into her chair.

"Do you think this is a game?" she demanded quietly. "Do you think I agreed to instruct you in the Craft just so you could fritter away your talent on some little boy? We are after an imp here, Rosamunde Rivera. An unpredictable creature who can go from being merely obnoxious to downright dangerous at the drop of a hat. He's out there, somewhere, and we let him go. Now it's up to us, and only us, to catch him."

Unable to meet her mother's blazing eyes, Rosie dropped hers and swallowed hard. It took her awhile to speak. What she finally said was "Let's go watch the news."

But as the anchors and reporters blathered on about oil cartels, Senate debates, international drug busts, and military coups, Rosie found her mind drifting. She wondered if Johnny would mind seeing her in the same outfit she'd worn to school and if her mother would holler at her again when she left for her date.

The phone rang, interrupting her thoughts. She sprang up. Lydia gently, but firmly, pushed her back down. "I'll get it," she said. "You keep watching."

Rosie sighed.

". . . no one knows how long the temporary cease-fire will last," the newscaster finished, then turned to her partner, a dapper man in his forties with dark hair and tan skin, both of which looked molded out of plastic.

"Poltergeists in a TV studio? That was one of the explanations offered for today's strange happenings on the set of "Down the Drain," this network's popular sitcom about two sewer workers and their pet alligator, Pig. Rhonda Marcus has the story."

Rosie's ears pricked up. She leaned forward, suddenly interested.

An attractive red-haired reporter stood on an empty soundstage. "Everything's quiet now here in Studio C on the Cosmopolitan Studios lot. But just a few hours ago, in front of over three hundred eyewitnesses and rolling TV cameras, the scene here could only be described as mayhem."

The reporter's voice continued over footage taken by the sitcom's cameramen.

"First the dummy pipes that are part of the set began to rumble. Next they began to flood. Then scores of baby crocodilians streamed across the stage and into the audience, causing mass panic."

Rosie's eyes widened as the cameras showed hundreds of people jumping out of their seats and screaming down the aisles.

"Forty-seven people had to be treated for minor injuries resulting from the human stampede. Miraculously, no one was seriously hurt. What could have caused these events?

The police are investigating but have released no further information as yet. We asked several eyewitnesses their theories."

"It was nuts. People running all over the place. Some nasty prankster must have done this," one of the lead actors said.

"An angry employee," said a stagehand.

"A publicity stunt that backfired," a middle-aged spectator suggested.

"A poltergeist." Three teenage boys grinned.

"Uh . . . maybe it was . . . uh . . . some kind of a mistake," stammered a boy, age twelve or so, standing there with his younger sister. They both looked troubled. The girl tugged the boy away from the camera.

Rosie stared at the back of his baseball jacket. Stitched across it was a word. "P-A-U-L-I-N-G," Rosie read. "Pauling. Pauling! Mom! Mom!"

Lydia came into the room.

"The TV . . . news . . . It's got to be . . . Here . . . Here." Rosie excitedly fumbled with the VCR, turning off the timer, rewinding the tape. Without letting her mother say a word, Rosie showed her the report and froze the picture on the boy's back.

"Look. Pauling. L.A. The imp. Those snowstorms. It all fits."

"Yes." Lydia nodded. "It fits." Her voice was calm, but her eyes were gleaming with excitement.

"Now we can call the L.A. directory and try to find their phone number."

"I don't think that will be necessary."

"Why?"

Lydia smiled, a full-blown smile she saved only for special occasions. "Because that was Adam Pauling on the phone. He finally got our message and he's coming over here just as fast as possible. If anybody can lead us to his kids and that imp, he can."

Chapter Fourteen

I knew it. I knew he was getting out of hand," Laura whispered insistently, as she perched atop the toilet lid.

Danny shifted awkwardly on the cold, hard edge of the bathtub. He hated to admit it, but he was beginning to suspect his sister might be right—and she didn't even know about what had happened in his science class. The TV studio episode had convinced her. It had certainly gone beyond, way beyond, what Danny had planned.

He'd suggested to the imp a little water in the actors' faces—just a small splash, really, no serious harm intended. And he'd asked to see Pig, who was a puppet, come alive. The last thing he'd wanted was a flood of water and alligators, followed by mass panic.

"We can't let him do any more crazy stuff," Laura went on.

And even though Danny reckoned she might also be correct about that, he felt irked—by her tone, by the way she'd strong-armed him into the bathroom to prevent the imp from overhearing. So, perversely, he said, "Oh, come on. He was just having fun. Nobody really got hurt."

"No thanks to him. Did you see that little girl with the braids? She was terrified."

Danny hadn't seen her. But he'd noticed an elderly man who was having trouble getting out of his seat. Three people had stepped on his feet before someone finally helped him up and out of the studio. Danny had the awful feeling he'd dream of that man tonight. He let out his breath slowly. "Look, I'll talk to him. I'll tell him we have to make some rules—"

"What makes you think he's going to listen to your rules?" Laura cut in.

"Of course he'll listen," Danny snapped. "I'm his boss, remember?"

"I wouldn't be too sure of that."

Stung, Danny jumped to his feet. "Yeah? You watch me."

He threw open the bathroom door and went into his room, the last place he'd left the imp, with Laura trailing behind. But Mr. Ed was no longer there. Nor was he in Laura's room. They found him instead in Ginny's, where he had just changed her expensive perfume into Essence of Wet Dog. Now he'd progressed to the rest of her cosmetics. His fingers working overtime, he was changing the colors from pleasant pinks and reds to ghastly greens and bilious yellows, then trying the powders and creams on his own face to appreciate the effect.

"We need to talk," Danny said to him, with no preamble.

Mr. Ed smeared on some marigold orange eye shadow and batted his lids in the mirror. " 'Oh, you beautiful doll, you great big beautiful doll,' " he sang to his reflection.

"What happened at the TV studio must never happen again."

"You're wonderful, gorgeous, sensational, pulchritudinous, adorable. You're a babe." The imp put on a slash of chartreuse lipstick and blew himself a kiss.

"From now on, no more improvising. You'll do what I say and nothing else."

Still singing, Mr. Ed opened Ginny's closet and took out several hats, which he proceeded to shoot around the room like flying saucers.

"You got that?" Danny demanded, grabbing a flowered hat right out of the imp's hands.

A nasty look scuttled over Mr. Ed's face—the same look Laura had seen fleetingly once before. This time Danny saw it as well. It made his heart pound briefly and sickeningly.

Then the imp flashed his familiar ingratiating grin. "Danny boy," he said smoothly in an Irish brogue. "You're starting to sound like a wet blanket. A party pooper. A stick-in-the-mud. A flat tire. A drip, a pill, a stiff. A crashing bore, if you get my drift."

Danny swallowed. This wasn't going the way he wanted it to. "Well . . . well . . . ," he stammered. Come on, he told himself. Why are you letting him get to you? Who cares what he says? You're still the boss. Making his voice as cool as possible, he said, "Frankly, Mr. Ed, your opinion of me isn't worth diddlysquat. Your job is to listen and obey. And if you can't do that, maybe it's time to send you back where you came from." He stuck out his chin and stared hard at the imp.

Next to him, Laura winced. She had the distinct feeling the imp would laugh off that last challenge—especially since they didn't know just where he came from or how to send him back there.

To her surprise, Mr. Ed didn't laugh. He began to cry. Tears gushed down his cheeks. "Oh, oh, oh," he wailed. "And here I thought we were friends, pals, buddies, true blues, partners."

Danny was taken aback. It was impossible to believe the imp. But he was weeping so hard and he seemed so sincere it was impossible not to. Danny had the uncontrollable urge to pat him on the shoulder. He reached out his hand. Laura smacked it away. She was finding the imp easier and easier to resist.

Mr. Ed grinned at her. "Can't blame me for trying," he said, tossing a straw hat with big fake roses onto Laura's head.

The roses turned real. She could smell their fragrance. Now it was her turn to be surprised. Why would the imp do anything nice for her? Suddenly she heard a faint buzzing. Confused, she turned toward the open window. In the distance she could see a small dark cloud. It was moving closer and closer to the house, and with it the buzzing grew louder and louder. It took Laura a moment to realize what was causing it. Bees—heading straight for the open window and her head.

She shrieked and tore out of the room. Behind her she

heard Danny yell, "Stop it! You promised never to hurt her or me."

"I lied," came the imp's cheerful reply.

The bees poured into the room and Danny took off after his sister, slamming the door behind him.

Without thinking clearly, they headed for the front door, flung it open, and nearly collided with their mother, who was just coming up the steps. They hadn't even heard her car pull up—the bees had drowned out its rumble.

"What's the matter? Why are you home from school already? Where are you two headed like a house afire? It isn't on fire, is it?" Ginny stared fearfully at her home.

"No," Laura panted, quivering and looking behind her. "Not . . . on . . . fire."

"Teachers' conference." Danny's lie came out in a gasp. "Why are . . . *you* home . . . already?" His glance anxiously followed his sister's, and his hands kept clenching and unclenching.

"There was a problem with the electricity today. The lights went off," Ginny answered.

Both of her children turned their heads again as if they were being pursued.

"What's the matter? Are you all right?"

"Yes," said Danny.

"No," answered Laura.

He shot her a warning look.

Ginny was instantly suspicious. "What's going on in there?" She charged past them into the house.

"Wait, Mom!" Laura called, torn as to whether or not to follow.

Danny grabbed her arm. "Don't you dare tell her a

thing," he ordered in a hoarse whisper. Swallowing his own fear, he pulled her along after their mother.

Trembling, Laura kept mum as her mother walked in and out of the rooms, checking to see if anything was amiss. But when they reached Ginny's room, she could keep quiet no longer. "Mom, don't go in there!" she shouted.

"Why not?" Ginny demanded.

"Because . . . because . . ."

"Bees," Danny explained, sounding much calmer than he felt. "Somehow a swarm of bees got into the house, into your room."

Ginny put her ear to the door. "I don't hear any buzzing," she said, and she opened it.

"Oh no!" Laura cried twice, first in fright, then in amazement. Not only were the bees gone but the hats, the cosmetics, and everything else the imp had strewn about the room were in place. Furthermore, the window was shut.

"The bees, they must have left," Danny offered with as much conviction as he could muster.

"And closed the window behind them?" Ginny raised an eyebrow.

Danny and Laura didn't respond.

Their mother inspected her room, but again she found nothing out of order. Danny tugged his sister's arm and began to lead her out the door. Ginny stopped them. "Wait a second. Wait just one second. Just what exactly have you been up to today?"

"Nothing," Danny told her. "Just the bees—"

Standing straight and defiant, Laura interrupted. "Tell her the truth, Danny. It's time. Tell her—or I will."

"Shut up," he hissed.

"Tell me *what?*" Ginny demanded.

When Danny refused to speak, Laura did. "Mom . . . we have a genie."

"Jeannie? Who's she?"

"It's a he. His name is Mr. Ed, and he came in one of Dad's Christmas presents."

"Cute, Laura. Very cute. But aren't you a little old for this sort of thing?"

"What sort of thing?"

"An imaginary playmate."

"He's not imaginary. He's real. Danny, tell her."

Danny punched her arm.

"Oww." She hit him back.

Then they fell on the floor, wrestling.

"Stop that! Stop that now!" Ginny yelled, trying, without success, to separate them.

"Allow me," someone boomed.

Ginny looked up into the blue eyes and big teeth of the imp. "Oh, my God!" she screamed. "Who are you? Where did you come from?"

He plucked Laura by her collar and Danny by his and shook them in the air. "They call me a genie. But my correct title is *Impus mischievous.*"

"I don't care if your correct title is *Canis Major.* Put my kids down."

"Gladly." Mr. Ed dropped them on the bed.

"Who is this man?" Ginny asked her children.

"Mr. Ed," they chorused.

"He's a friend of yours?"

"Not anymore," Danny swore.

"Okay. Then, will *you* ask him to leave or shall *I?*"

Danny had not thought of this possibility before. Straightening his shirt, he looked at the imp and said as forcefully as he could, "I want you to leave. Immediately."

"Uh-uh. Not likely," the imp replied.

"What do you mean not likely? Who *are* you?" Ginny demanded.

"I told you who I am. They told you what to call me. And I mean not likely, because I like it here."

"I'm calling the police."

"I wouldn't if I were you."

"Try and stop me," said Ginny, reaching for the phone.

"Okay," said the imp. He waved his hands and Ginny Pauling disappeared.

"Mom!" screamed Laura.

"Bring her back. Now!" Danny commanded.

"No, I don't think so, *boss*." The imp drawled out the last word. "I'm not in the mood." Then he sat down at Ginny's dresser, picked up a file, and began doing his nails.

Chapter Fifteen

Danny! Laura!" Adam Pauling exclaimed, as he watched his children on tape. For a moment he forgot that he thought the woman sitting next to him was nuts, no matter how calm and dignified she appeared—and that he himself had to be crazy, too, for actually coming over to her house. "I don't believe it!" he called out, quite astonished. "They're on TV!" There was a note of amused pride in his voice.

Lydia took him to task for it. "Mr. Pauling, your children are the pawns of a malicious spirit. It's fortunate neither they nor anyone else was seriously hurt by him—this time."

Adam flushed with irritation. "Yes, it *is* lucky they weren't hurt. But what makes you so all-fired certain this imp of yours is mixed up with my kids?" He stopped short of adding, "If there is such a thing as an imp, which I seriously doubt."

Lydia looked at her daughter. "It all fits, Mr. Pauling," Rosie explained, expanding on what her mother had already told him earlier on the phone. "The incidents, the mischief, the means of escape. He tied me up in the basement, then went up to the shop and waited on you. Then he disappeared. We sealed off everything in the shop, but he got away—in one of the gifts you sent your kids."

Adam took a deep breath to settle himself. "And what's your stake in all this," he asked reasonably.

"The same as yours, Mr. Pauling. We want to protect your children—and others—from harm," Lydia answered. "We also feel responsible for unleashing this creature into the world. We want to put him back where he came from."

"And that was?"

"A bottle in the basement," Rosie replied.

Adam coughed. These people really *are* lunatics, he thought.

But he didn't make a move toward the door.

"Have you called your children yet?" Lydia put in.

"I tried just after I spoke to you. The line was busy."

"Then may I suggest you try again now."

Pushy, aren't you, Adam thought. But he said, "Sure, why not?" and picked up the phone.

This time it rang only once before Laura answered. She sounded out of breath. "Hello . . . Pauling residence."

"Laura? Is that you?"

"Dad? Oh, Dad!" Her wail was so piercing even Lydia

and Rosie could hear it. "Help us! You've got to help! He's made Mom disappear. He won't let us leave. He . . ."

"Mr. Pauling!" a new voice interrupted. "What a delight to speak with you again. You were my very favorite customer. My only customer, but my favorite nonetheless."

"It's him!" Adam hissed, handing over the receiver. "The crazy guy who was in your store."

Lydia and Rosie nodded grimly.

"I like your children, too," the imp went on. "Or at least I did until they forgot their manners. They're still as cute as puppies, though. I may fit them with collars and take them for walks."

In his lifetime Adam prided himself on having dealt well with all kinds of difficult clients and situations over the telephone. But this was different. This wacko, this, if Lydia and Rosie were to be believed, *imp* was someone Adam had no idea how to handle.

"I'd like you to put my daughter or my son on the phone now," he said.

"They're busy working on a math problem. How many cockroaches does it take to fill up a bathtub?"

Adam heard shrieks and gagging noises in the background. "Then let me speak to my wife." He realized his blunder a second before the imp did.

"Your wife? Nobody here fits that description."

"My ex-wife," Adam said painfully. "Ginny."

"Like I said, nobody here fits that descrip-tion. . . . Well, it's been lovely chatting with you. Have a good wife."

"No. Wait. Don't go . . .," Adam begged.

115

The imp hung up.

Trembling with anxiety, Adam turned to Lydia and Rosie. "I've got to go to California. At once."

"We'll come with you," said Lydia.

"You? What for? What can you do?"

"I told you, Mr. Pauling. We're going to capture that imp so he can't cause any more trouble."

"How? How are you going to do that?"

"With magic," Rosie told him.

"Magic?"

"We're witches, Mr. Pauling."

"Ha." Adam barked out a short, hard laugh. "Ha ha ha. Now I've heard everything." He started for the door.

"My daughter can be a little crass, Mr. Pauling," Lydia called out. "But she does tell the truth." She muttered something under her breath.

Adam reached for the doorknob and found it kept slipping out of his grasp. He turned and stared at Lydia and Rosie, his eyes panicky. "This is a madhouse!"

"No. I assure you we're quite sane. We're all going to leave together, Mr. Pauling. And I promise you, we'll do everything we can to get your children out of the clutches of that imp."

Adam wasn't sure whether it was the sincerity in her voice or the fact that his feet seemed riveted to the floor, but in any case he decided he was licked. "All right. All right. But hurry. Hurry!"

Nine and a half minutes later, the three of them were on their way to the airport.

And three streets away, Johnny Haines, frowning down at a cold pizza, was stood up for the first time in his life.

Chapter Sixteen

"Yiii!" Laura yelled, sitting bolt upright and clapping her hands over her ears.

"Argh!" Danny cried, just as inarticulately, as he fell off the couch on which he and his sister had been allowed to share an unmercifully brief sleep.

Two feet away from them, dressed in scoutmaster regalia, Mr. Ed was blowing reveille on a battered bugle.

"Rise and shine, rise and shine," he commanded, lowering the instrument. "Now, repeat after me, 'I promise to be trustworthy, helpful, loyal, friendly, courteous, kind, obedient, cheerful, thrifty, brave, clean, and irrelevant.' "

Rubbing the elbow he'd just bruised, and still reverberating from the imp's wake-up call, Danny snapped, "Oh, bug off, will you!" The imp had been tormenting him and his sister almost all night long, and he showed no signs of letting up.

Tossing away his bugle, Mr. Ed said, "Bug off? Can't bug off without a bug to begin with." He twitched his fingers, and an enormous spider scuttled toward them. Danny and Laura screamed. Mr. Ed twitched his fingers again, and the spider vanished. "Bug offed." The imp bowed. Then he jumped upright. "Okeydokey. Let's go! Hup-two-three-four. Hup-two-three-four. . . ." He waggled his hands, and immediately Danny and Laura, dressed respectively in Boy and Girl Scout uniforms, were on their feet. Mr. Ed pivoted neatly and began marching toward the door.

"Wh-where are we going?" Laura stammered without following him.

"Ah, glad you asked." He turned back, marching in place. "We're going off to experience the beauty of nature, the majesty of the mountains, the universality of the eucalyptus, the good-grief-is-that-a-skunkness of the air. We're going to Spitzer's Camp."

"Spitzer's Camp!" Danny exclaimed.

It had been one of the first places Ginny had taken them to when they'd arrived in California. She'd read about it in a hiking book. She'd wanted to show them that L.A. wasn't all flat and sleek, that, like Vermont, it had interesting curves.

Danny had actually been quite impressed with the hills and canyons. He wouldn't admit it then, though. Instead, he'd said they looked naked without snow. But a few days ago, when the imp was still under control—or, at least, Danny thought he was—Danny had mentioned the camp, saying it would be fun to go there again and alter the environment to his satisfaction. Now it was the last place in the world he wanted to visit.

"We don't want to go to Spitzer's Camp," he declared, as firmly as he could.

"Now, now, now," the imp chided, looking down at him with blazing eyes. "Who's being a wimp, a schnook, a lazy boy, a wuss? Hmmm?"

Danny found himself on his knees, sucking his thumb.

"Uh, Mr. Ed," Laura said tremulously. "I have to . . . I need to go to the bathroom."

"Well, all right," the imp granted. "But make it snappy."

She nodded and rushed out of the room.

A few moments later, shaking, she stared at herself in the bathroom mirror. He's kidnapping us, she thought. He's made Mom disappear, and now we'll disappear, too, and no one will ever find us. Her lips began to quiver. She bit them. Don't. It won't do any good, she told herself. You have to be tough now, Laura. You just have to be.

She washed her face and hands and brushed her teeth, which felt like fur in her mouth. Then, just as she was about to leave, an idea came to her. She seized a bar of soap and with it scrawled "Spitzer's Camp" across the mirror. "There," she said aloud, trying to fan the very tiny ember of comfort she felt into a cheery blaze. Then she took a deep breath and strode out of the room.

"Look at those jagged mountains. Smell that crisp, clean air. It makes you feel strong, adventurous, hardy, manly, boyly, girly. It makes you want to sing!" The imp threw back his head and let out a yodel that started a small rockslide down the path.

"Watch out!" Danny cried, jumping up from the boulder on which he was sitting.

The imp turned and gave him a baleful look. "Watch out, *what*?" he asked.

Danny swallowed the lump in his throat along with his pride. "Watch out, boss," he mumbled sullenly.

"Louder. I can't hear you."

"Watch out, *boss*," Danny barked.

"That's better." The imp patted him on the head. "Now, get down and do fifty-nine and a half push-ups. Give you some spine. Toughen you up. Put some hair on your chest. Make a man out of you. You, too, honey bun." He pointed at Laura.

She and her brother stood there, arms folded, unmoving. They were tired, so tired that they were feeling mutinous.

"Come on. Hop to it." The imp made a funny gesture at them, and, before they could protest, they were down on their hands and toes, pushing up and down.

"One, two, three, ten, sixteen, seventeen, thirty-five, forty, forty-five, ninety, five hundred and six. Seven, eleven, snake eyes, craps, you're out!" bellowed the imp. "Now we'll take a hike!"

Danny and Laura groaned.

"Softies!" Mr. Ed spat, and made them march up the path. "Sound off. One, two. Sound off, dog doo. Sound off, p. u.," he chanted over and over like a demented drill sergeant, driving them ahead, driving them crazy. "Over hill, over dale, we will hit the dusty trail, while the capons go rolling along . . ."

"*Caissons*, you moron," Danny muttered so the imp wouldn't hear.

Laura did, though, and smiled to show her solidarity with her brother.

But the smile made Danny, already miserable with guilt, feel worse than ever. "I'm sorry, Laura," he said. "I should have listened to you days ago. I should have listened to you *weeks* ago when you objected to bringing him home in the first place."

"Oh, Danny. I was just as fooled by him as you were. Just as fooled and just as excited. I wanted to do wild and crazy things, too, and I believed we could keep him under control. At least I wanted to believe it."

But Danny was inconsolable. He stopped walking and made Laura do the same. "Mr. Ed!" he called out firmly.

The imp turned. "Yes?"

"Look, you can keep me as your slave, but let Laura go."

"Okay," said the imp. He began to march again. "She can go."

"Did you hear that, Laura? You can leave," Danny said, wishing he'd thought of that idea earlier, while they were still at home.

"No." Laura shook her head.

"What do you mean, no? Don't argue. Get out of here! Now!"

"I said, no. We're in this together. I don't believe him, anyway. And where could I go? There's not a car in sight.

We're miles and miles from home. And I'd probably get killed trying to hitch."

Danny knew she was right. The hopelessness of their situation made him strike the nearest tree. He grunted but refused to cry out when he skinned his knuckles. He stuck them in his mouth to stop the bleeding and fell into step once more behind Mr. Ed.

It seemed as though they walked for hours. But they always ended up back where they began. They'd arrived at the camp with its lone picnic table for the tenth time when at last the imp tired of the game and let them collapse onto a boulder. Then he scrambled up a cliff and beat his chest like Tarzan.

Danny and Laura leaned against each other, too exhausted to speak. Then Danny thought of something. "Do you think Dad will fly out here to find out what happened to us?"

"Yes," Laura answered without hesitation. "I bet he's here already."

"He'll never find us at this place, though. He'll arrive at our house and nobody will be there and he won't know where to go."

"Yes, he will." Laura dropped her voice to a whisper. "I left a message on the bathroom mirror."

"*You did?*"

"Shh. Yes. All Dad will need to find this place is a map."

Danny's eyes lit up with optimism. But just as quickly, they grew dull with despair. "Even if he does find us— even if we're still here by the time he shows up—what's to stop Mr. Ed from making *him* disappear, too, just like Mom?"

That was something Laura couldn't answer. She hadn't thought about it, hadn't wanted to think about it. And now that Danny had forced her to, she looked the way her old doll Betsy had looked the day he'd removed half its stuffing. "I hope Mommy is all right, wherever she is," she said, her voice quavering. Once again she tried to hold back the tears. But this time she failed.

It was Danny's turn to try and comfort her. But she only cried harder, until the imp let out an earsplitting whistle.

They jerked and stared at him.

He was standing at the very edge of the cliff, holding his arms out into space. "Top of the world, Ma!" he bellowed and jumped off.

They rushed over to look.

"Fooled you!" Mr. Ed chortled, hopping up from the impossibly small ledge below.

"You horrible creature!" Laura yelled, trying in vain to hit him. "You demon!"

"Some people don't know how to take a joke," the imp sniffed. Then he whirled around, changed two nearby rabbits into kangaroos, and imitated them as they hopped away.

Danny sat down again on the rock. He didn't have his watch on, but he guessed it was about nine o'clock in the morning. His stomach grumbled. Mr. Ed had given them no time to eat breakfast. He looked around. There were probably all kinds of edible things here, but he didn't know what they were. He felt sorry that he'd never taken wilderness survival training. It seemed more and more likely they were going to need it.

Laura came over and handed him an apple.

"Where'd you get this?" he asked.

"Brought it from home. I have another one, too, and some rolls. There's a bottle of water back in the trunk of the car, if you're thirsty."

Danny looked at his sister with new admiration and also embarrassment. And I thought I was the leader, the boss, he said to himself. Not only did I get us into all this trouble, but if it were up to me, we'd starve. "Let's split it." He cut the apple in half with his pocketknife. "We don't know how long our food will have to last."

"You're right," Laura agreed.

Sitting side by side, shoulders touching, they chewed the fruit slowly, appreciatively.

The imp had wandered off somewhere. They couldn't see him, but they knew he was around. There were traces of him everywhere—a group of trees that had become giant umbrellas, a stream that turned first to mud, then to gold.

"Some of it *was* fun, wasn't it?" Danny said wistfully, staring at the sky.

As if in answer, it began to snow. They watched it come down, softly, gently, both of them wondering sorrowfully why things had to go so awry.

Suddenly, Laura sat up. "Do you hear something?"

"What?" asked Danny.

"Something like a motor . . . like a car."

Danny listened. "No. I don't hear anything."

Laura sighed. "It must have been my imagination."

Danny nodded.

"What do you think he plans to do with us?" she said after a pause, begging her brother for an answer that would ease her fear.

Danny wished he could give her one, but he couldn't. "I don't know," he replied. Then he turned his head. "The car. Now I hear it."

"It's not ours, is it? He's not driving away and leaving us here!" Laura clutched his arm.

Terrified, they bolted down the path to the tiny parking lot. But the Thunderbird was sitting cold and quiet, exactly where they'd left it. Mr. Ed was still nowhere in sight. And the hum of an engine was now clear and close.

"Stop!" Danny and Laura began to shout before they could see the car. "Stop! Help us! Stop!" They ran out to the road, yelling and waving as a rented blue Taurus chugged into view. It stopped without even bothering to reach the lot. The door flew open, and out flew Adam Pauling.

"Dad!" Danny and Laura shouted, running into his arms. Over his shoulder they saw a woman and a girl they didn't recognize.

"Let's go," Adam said, pulling them toward the car. "You, too," he told Lydia and Rosie.

"No, Mr. Pauling. You know we can't just leave. We have to deal with the imp," Lydia told him.

"The hell with the imp! I've got my children. Let's go!"

"But Mom . . . ," said Laura.

Adam froze. "Where is she?"

"We don't know, Dad," Danny said. "He really did make her disappear."

Laura started to cry again.

"Well, where is he, that wacko? I'll kill him."

"No, you won't, Mr. P.," said Rosie. "You can't. You go sit in the car with your kids and leave this to us."

Adam paused, then turned toward the automobile. It began to roll backward, slowly at first, but then picking up speed. He raced after it and caught up with the car just as it stopped at a guardrail. But just as he reached out toward it, the Taurus sprang into the air like a wallaby, did a somersault, and tumbled right over the cliff and out of sight.

"Oh, my Lo-Lord," Adam stammered. "What . . . what do I d-do now?"

Mr. Ed jumped down from a eucalyptus tree and landed right in front of him. "If I were you," he said matter-of-factly, "I'd get a horse."

Chapter Seventeen

"So nice to see you all again—or to meet you." The imp bowed to Lydia. "Let's see now . . . one, two, three, four, five, six . . . just the right number for a picnic." He danced back up to the campsite with everyone following.

"I've prepared a delightful spread." He waved at the picnic table, which was immediately covered with plates, cups, and bowls of varying sizes. "We have . . ."—he began throwing the lids off the containers—"fish heads in cream. Spaghetti and slugs. Potato salad and cold sores. Deviled legs. Ham-and-fleas sandwiches. And Jell-O mold. Come on, now, and eat up. No dessert until you've finished every bite."

Everyone turned somewhat green, except for Lydia, who took out from her satchel a large, plain brown glass bottle and set it on the ground between herself and the imp.

"Ah, a beverage, a libation, a potable, a drink. How thoughtful."

"Beverage, my aunt Fanny. Don't you recognize it?" Rosie called out. "It's your home, sweet home."

Lydia gave her a disapproving glance. Rosie returned it with a semiapologetic shrug. She couldn't help it, really. Seeing the imp again reminded her of how he'd tormented her—albeit for a relatively brief time. She wanted to see him get what he deserved—and that was to see him disappear, period.

"My home, eh." The imp walked over to the bottle. "Well. Well, well, well, well, well." He squatted down, pressed one eye to the top, and peered inside. "How nice of you to have kept everything just as I left it. It touches me deeply. It really does." He beamed at Lydia and Rosie.

They did not smile back. Lydia stood wary, but not tense—a cat on the alert. Rosie tried to imitate her mother, but her fingers kept fidgeting with the amulet around her neck.

"Who are they, Dad?" Laura whispered. "And what are they doing?"

"Shh," Adam shushed her. He didn't want to draw any more of the imp's attention to himself or to his children, if he could help it.

"The only problem is," Mr. Ed continued, ignoring them, "this home was, is, and always will be . . . for the birds." He twitched his shoulders twice and shot out his pinkies three times, and all at once, it began to rain eggs. Big eggs, little eggs, fresh eggs, rotten eggs. Where they came from was anybody's guess, but down they came.

Rosie dodged as many as she could. Danny, Laura, and

Adam crawled under the picnic table to weather the storm. But Lydia stood stalwart, yellow yolk running down her face.

"Let he who troubles me be bound with the Invisible Net," she declared, her voice echoing through the canyons. Reaching into her pocket, she drew out and tossed a pinch of cinnabar, dried honey, and powdered spiderwebs along with flash paper on the ground. The flash paper made a small, but dramatic, explosion.

At once, the eggs stopped pelting them, the nasty food disappeared from the tabletop, and the imp, arms at his sides, legs pressed tightly together, struggled in place like a creature tied with unseen cords.

"It worked!" Rosie cried out, stunned.

"Wow!" Laura exclaimed at the same time. "They must be witches!"

Danny scrambled out from under the table. "How did you do that?" he asked.

But it was the imp who thought he was being addressed. He flourished his hand in the air. "Acting!" he declaimed and took a bow. "Now, run on back to your daddy. It's what you've wanted to do all along, anyway." He flicked his thumb at Danny, and the boy stumbled backward against his father, who had been standing some six feet behind him.

"Leave him alone!" Adam yelled.

"Sure. Why not? That's what you've done for years, isn't it?" Mr. Ed grinned.

Adam winced and laid his hand on his son's shoulder. But Danny ducked away from it.

"Don't let him get to you," said Laura.

"It didn't work," Rosie moaned. She looked at her mother. "*Why* didn't it work?"

Lydia didn't answer her. His power *has* grown. This is going to be harder than I thought, she realized, but she didn't want to announce the fact. Instead, she concentrated on thinking of another spell to try on the imp.

"I'll tell you why it didn't work." Mr. Ed waltzed in front of Rosie. "It didn't work because you're incompetent. Inept. Incapable. Maladroit. Bungling. Stupid. Asinine. Dumb. In short, as witches, you stink. . . ."

"We do not!" Rosie shouted.

"And also because you don't know my real name."

"What? What are you talking about?"

"Remember Rumpelstiltskin?" the imp explained. "The miller's daughter couldn't get rid of him until she found out his real name. Same is true for me."

"You mean your name isn't really Mr. Ed?" added Danny.

"Or Amenhotep?" Laura called out.

"No sirree, Bob." The imp grinned, clicking his teeth rapidly like a windup set of dentures.

Rosie turned to Lydia. "Mom, is this true?"

"Possibly," she answered.

"Possibly! How come you didn't mention this before?"

"I thought it was an old wives' tale."

Rosie groaned. "How are we going to figure out his real name?"

"Is it Damian?" asked Laura, temporarily forgetting her fear.

"Nope," said the imp.

"Beelzebub?" suggested Danny.

"Uh-uh."

"Mordred? Ozzie? Puck? Stinky? Dave?"

"No, no, no, no, no," the imp sang.

"Look, he might be putting us on. This name stuff might be baloney," said Lydia. "And besides, even if it isn't, there's more than one way to catch an imp. Now, ignore him and work the Silver Spiral."

"The Silver Spiral," the imp scoffed. "A cheap trick used by amateurs. Let's put it to use, shall we? Let's see if it can protect you against this—Ka-choo, ka-choo, ka-choo!" He made a series of chopping gestures.

Everyone but Lydia and Laura looked up at the sky, nervously expecting more eggs or something worse to come pouring down. Lydia kept her eyes on the imp. Laura glanced sideways, so it was she who saw the twenty-two pairs of skierless skis and ski poles come slaloming down the mountain at them.

"Look out!" she yelled, dragging her father and her brother back under the table. Six pairs of skis (and three poles) flew over it. The poles thumped so hard on the tabletop they nearly pierced the wood.

Six other pairs of skis whizzed past Rosie on either side of her. The wind they raised spun her around. She fought to keep concentrating on the spiral, but what had been so easy in her basement proved to be a lot less so there in the San Gabriel Mountains with a mad imp on the loose.

Only Lydia was unmoved—even when the remaining ten pairs threatened to crash right into her. Her spiral deflected them neatly, and as they soared harmlessly over her head, she spat on the ground three times and uttered, "You are unwelcome here, *Impus mischievous*. Whittle away, whittle away. Go into your bottle where you will stay." Then she repeated the spell backward, "Stay will you where bottle your into go. Away whittle, away whittle. *Mischievous Impus*, here unwelcome are you."

The imp hopped onto the bottle. "Help me! I'm melting!" he cried as he began to shrink down into it. First his legs disappeared, then his torso, then his arms. When only his head remained in sight, Rosie rushed forward with the stopper.

"I'm melting," whimpered the imp. Then he looked at Rosie and blew a stream of water into her face.

"Eww," she yelled, and stepped back as he popped out of the bottle.

"Fool you once, shame on me. Fool you twice, shame on you," he taunted, jumping up on the picnic table and doing a wild flamenco.

The Paulings cowered beneath him, covering their ears.

Mr. Ed stuck his head over the side. "And how are we doing down there? Practicing a little family togetherness, I see. Too bad Mommy's missing. You'd like her back, wouldn't you, Danny boy?"

Danny was pale and shaky. "Yes," he said hoarsely.

"Believe it or not, so would your dad. Wouldn't you, Adam?"

"Stop it!" Adam ordered. "Stop playing games and bring her back!"

"If you want her to come back so much, why'd you let her go in the first place?" asked the imp.

"I don't know."

"All this really is your fault then, isn't it?" Mr. Ed smiled.

"No," Adam protested.

"Yes, it is!" yelled Danny.

"No, it isn't. It's Mom's fault! She *wanted* to leave Dad—and Vermont," Laura burst out, shocking herself. Up until that moment, she'd had no idea she felt that angry.

"Don't blame your mother," Adam scolded. "She tried to tell me how she was feeling, but I didn't listen—"

"She didn't listen to you, either," Laura insisted.

"And neither of you ever listened to us," Danny shouted.

"Peace. Harmony. Goodwill toward men!" the imp cackled, jumping off the table and doing a jig.

"Mom, we've got to do something," said Rosie, growing more and more unnerved by the imp's antics (and the Paulings' arguments). "You must know some other spell that will work."

"Stay calm, Rosie," said Lydia, collecting her strength.

" 'I want to be happy, but I won't be happy, till I make you happy, too . . . ,' " sang Mr. Ed, his jig having turned into a soft shoe.

". . . and you kept watching TV!" Danny bellowed.

". . . and she walked out of the room!" Laura shrieked.

". . . and before I knew it, you were all gone!" Adam howled, toppling over the picnic table.

"I want to flatten him!" Rosie growled. "And them, too," she added in an aside.

Mr. Ed heard her. "Why, what an inspired idea," he said, beating his fists on his thighs.

"Wait," Rosie pleaded with a sinking feeling. "What are you do—"

The rest of her sentence was cut off by the scrape and rumble of shifting rock. Around her and her companions, the pebbles, the boulders, the mountains themselves began to tremble.

Rosie turned ashen. "Mom, he's going to cause an avalanche," she rasped.

"Oh no, he won't," Lydia declared. "Ammomgib will stop him." She narrowed her eyes at the imp.

He made a sound like a small yelp.

Lydia heard it and smiled boldly.

"Am-am-mong-gib?" Rosie stuttered, taken aback by the smile. "What's that?"

"Weren't you paying attention when I told you about her? Or were you too busy thinking about someone else?" Lydia said, annoyed. "She's the Queen of the Genies. And we're going to summon her. Now!"

"No!" Mr. Ed snapped. "You can't!"

"Oh yes, we can," Lydia told him. "Come here, Rosie."

Now it was Rosie's turn to gasp. She suddenly recalled not only the spirit, but what Lydia had said about summoning her: "It's dangerous. If we don't do it exactly right, it will backfire, and we will end up as her slaves."

"Mom, are you sure . . . ," Rosie began.

"Rosamunde, come over here at once!" Lydia ordered.

Rosie gulped and ran over to her mother, who was pacing a circle around them and dropping nettle leaves, myrrh gum, and feathers as she walked.

"Power is as power be. Ammomgib, we conjure thee.

Not in malice, not in fear, but to help our cause we draw you near," she recited.

"No!" the imp hollered again. "Never! Not! Nyet! Uh-uh! Forget it! You lose!" He pounded his fists against each other and stomped on the ground. The mountains shuddered. Across the way a cliff crumbled and fell. The picnic table jiggled along the ground until it tumbled into a crevasse and wedged there like a splinter in a giant's big toe.

Laura screamed and clutched hold of her father. Adam searched frantically for somewhere else they could hide, but he found no place. Danny turned to run and suddenly stopped, Lydia's voice ringing in his ears.

"We to master, you to aid. The circle waits. The circle's laid," she went on, ignoring everything but the spell. "By the left, by the right. By the tongue, by the hand. You must serve while we com . . . Oh!" Lydia's face went blank with surprise as the ground split open under her feet. She leapt to avoid falling into the crack and succeeded, but she lost her balance and fell, striking her head on a rock.

"Mom?" Rosie bent down and shook her gently. "Mom? Lydia?"

There was no response. She was out cold.

"Oh no," Rosie began to sob. "Oh no."

Around her the whole landscape was rippling and buckling like waves at sea. A hundred cracks slashed through the earth. Trees crashed all around her. And still the imp roared and stamped and pounded his fists.

"Don't. Don't cry. Finish it."

Rosie looked up. On the other side of the circle, Danny was watching her. "Finish what?" she sniffled.

"The spell. Hurry. You can do it."

"No, I can't remember . . ." She flushed. "I wasn't paying attention . . . There was this boy . . ."

"Yes, you can," Danny silenced her firmly but kindly. "Try."

Rosie stared at him, this unexpected ally, and saw desperation and bravery and understanding all mixed together in his face. I'm responsible for this, he was saying silently. So am I, she answered without words. And she knew she had to set things right.

"Okay. I'll try," she said. Mouth dry, she began haltingly to resume the spell. "By the left, by the right. By the tongue, by the hand. You must serve while we command. Uh . . . uh . . ." She strained to remember the final words. What were they? Something about goodwill. "For the . . . for the *good* of all." Yes, that's right. Go on. "For the . . . uh . . . *will* of all." Uh-huh. Keep going. "For the *strength* of all. So it must be." She wiped the sweat off her upper lip and rubbed her slippery palms together. Then, raising them high in the air, she invoked the Queen of the Genies: "Ammomgib, listen, hear. Ammomgib, you must appear!"

All at once, there was silence. The rocks, the trees, the ground stopped rolling and crashing. The imp vanished. And a beam of light fell in the exact center of the circle. Brighter and brighter it grew. Rosie had to close her eyes against it. But the light seared even through her lids. She crossed her arms over her face and moaned, "Stop. Go away. Go away."

"Go away? I just got here," said a deep female voice.

Carefully, Rosie lowered her arms. The light seemed bearable now. Slowly, she opened her eyes.

There, before her, was the tallest, roundest, greenest woman she'd ever seen in her life. "Ammomgib?" she squeaked.

The Queen of the Genies raised one bushy eyebrow. "You were perhaps expecting Madonna?" she said.

Rosie thought it best not to reply.

Chapter Eighteen

So, young lady, what is it you would have me do?" asked the Queen of the Genies.

"Um . . . oh . . . ," Rosie stammered, awed by her size and grandeur. She was dressed in a flowing robe that changed color with every shift of the light and had more gold and precious gems than Rosie had ever seen in her life. Even her yellow hair, which stood up straight as a haystack with not a straw out of place, was hung with jewels. One of them, a ruby as big as a plum tomato, dipped rakishly over her right eye.

Rosie couldn't take her eyes off it, until Danny cleared his throat behind her. "Oh yes. I want you to catch the imp and make sure he can do no more harm. And I order you to put everything back . . . in . . . uh . . . order."

Ammomgib inclined her massive head. Several olive-size emeralds fell off her neck into Rosie's hands. "Your wish is my command. Imp, show yourself!" the Queen ordered.

Mr. Ed did not appear.

"Hmmm." Ammomgib gave an annoyed grunt, which sounded to Rosie only a little softer than a furnace turning on right next to her ear. "Imp, I command you!"

But the creature stayed out of sight.

"He's stubborn," Rosie offered helpfully.

"Stubborn. I'll give him stubborn." Ammomgib took a deep breath and roared like a moose into a microphone on maximum volume, "Nasmodicon, you little whipper-snapper. If you don't get out here this minute, I'll tell your father and you'll be demoted to a mosquito!"

There was a crinkly noise as a reluctant cloud of smoke slowly funneled out of an old discarded Good & Plenty box. Ammomgib tapped her foot impatiently. Even Rosie got restless until finally the imp slunk out of the haze and into the circle, where he stood before Ammomgib, head hanging, mouth drooping, electric blue eyes looking like they needed new batteries.

"So," said the Queen of the Genies. "We think we're hot stuff, do we? We think we can cause a little earthquake, scare a bunch of people to pieces, take over the territory like some kind of high-and-mighty demon instead of just a puny little imp."

Mr. Ed—or Nasmodicon, as it turns out he was really named—shuffled uncomfortably.

"You're leaving with me now," Ammomgib went on. "A couple of classes in Mischief 101 or A.I.B. should do the trick."

"What's A.I.B.?" Rosie piped up.

"Appropriate Imp Behavior," answered Ammomgib, without taking her eyes off Nasmodicon. "If not," she said to him, "it's the Institute for you—you got that?"

"Yes," he muttered.

"Yes, *what?*"

"Yes, Mother."

"Mother?" chorused a stunned Rosie, Danny, and Laura, who was peeking out from behind her dad.

"What's the matter? Can't a genie be a mother?" Ammomgib chided them. "I'm a good one, too—even if this kid of mine and I haven't seen each other for a little while. Well, maybe a long while. But who's fault was that?" She glared at the imp. "If Mr. Too-Big-For-His-Britches here hadn't gotten into all that trouble years ago in Louisiana . . . The last straw was when he made the fishermen catch earmuffs instead of crabs. They called in a sorcerer. I see you have his bottle. Well, you won't need it anymore, I can promise you that." She snapped her fingers and the bottle disappeared.

Then, without warning, she turned back to the imp, who was beginning to tiptoe out of the circle. "Uh, uh, uh," she warned, snatching him back by the collar.

Nasmodicon sniffed. "You didn't have to do that. I wasn't going anywhere."

"Sure, you weren't." Ammomgib took his hand. "May we have permission to depart now?" she asked Rosie.

"Oh yes. Certainly. By all means," Rosie replied.

Without touching her, Rosie dropped the stones into her shovel-size hand.

"Thank you, my dear. You need help again, just call

on me. . . . But try not to do it in the near future. I don't like to overwork."

"Oh, don't worry. I won't," said Rosie, and she meant it.

Once again the bright light appeared. Just before Rosie had to shield her eyes, she caught a glimpse of the imp. He was still looking downcast. But then he glanced up and saw her, and he wiggled his eyebrows like Groucho Marx. Incorrigible, Rosie thought with a touch of amusement, and she raised her arm across her brow. When she was able to lower it, the imp and his mother were gone.

Rosie heaved a huge sigh. But her relief was short lived.

"Mom," she whispered. "Mom!" she cried, and knelt beside Lydia.

"Unnhhh," her mother groaned, blinking and twisting her head back and forth. With Rosie's support, she sat up.

"How are you?" Rosie asked.

"How is she?" Danny joined her.

"She's got a headache. But she'll live," answered Lydia, with a feeble smile.

"He's gone," said Laura to no one—and everyone. "I can't believe it. He's gone." Then she looked around nervously. "Isn't he?"

Danny put his arm around her. "Yes. He's gone."

He had a strange expression on his face. Sadder, but wiser? wondered Laura. Glad, but disappointed? She wasn't sure.

Lydia stood up, swaying slightly, and surveyed the landscape. The trees, the rocks, the cliffs were back in place; the earth was mended, as if it had never been broken. She turned to her daughter. "I take it that you succeeded in completing the spell."

Rosie nodded with both pride and shyness. "The Queen of the Genies, she was. . . ." She hesitated over the word.

"Awesome?" Lydia finished.

Rosie smiled. "Yeah. That's one way to describe her."

After a moment of quiet, Lydia said, "Well, I guess we ought to go back." She turned to look at Adam.

He was standing all alone, bewildered and forlorn. "Ginny?" he said, quizzically. "Where's Ginny?"

"Mom!" gasped Danny and Laura, shocked that they'd actually forgotten about their mother for a while.

"Oh no. He didn't bring her back." Laura's lip quivered.

"And his mother didn't make him." Danny's eyes began to water.

"I told her . . . I told her to set everything right. I thought that covered it all." Rosie, too, was suddenly on the verge of tears.

"Danny? Laura?"

They all heard the voice and spun around.

"That's Mom!" said Laura.

They looked left and right and into the canyons, but they couldn't see her.

"Where is she?" asked Danny.

"I'm here," Ginny answered, although she didn't sound all that certain herself.

"Look," said Rosie, pointing up at a eucalyptus.

There, in a crook between the largest branches, sat Ginny Pauling, a little disheveled and a lot confused but, in the opinion of her two children, looking better than she ever had in her whole life.

She shinnied down the trunk like an old hand at tree climbing and grabbed Danny and Laura in a bear hug.

"Where *were* you?" asked Laura, laughing and crying.

"I don't know, really," Ginny replied. "I was in a small green room somewhere. Every few minutes some woman with a clipboard, designer clothes, and a very expensive haircut would come in and say, 'And don't forget, you're on fourth.' It was very peculiar." Then she glanced up and saw Adam.

He was standing at the fringes of the reunion, unsure of how welcome he was to join in. "Hello, Ginny," he said. His eyes were very bright.

"Hello, Adam," she responded, without surprise.

"The kids called me," he explained anyway.

She nodded.

"And . . . and . . . I'm thinking of taking some time off so I can be with Danny and Laura and with you, and we can talk. What do you think about that?" It came out in a rush, startling Adam as much as Ginny.

She took her time answering. It was the look in Danny's and Laura's eyes—a hopeful, longing look—that convinced her at last. "Well," she said. "I think we could all use some time to talk."

She smiled at Adam. He smiled back. Danny and Laura cheered.

Watching the whole thing, Lydia mused aloud, "Nice family. I wonder if they would have gotten back together if it hadn't been for the imp."

"You mean I did a good thing after all, letting him out of the bottle?" asked Rosie, as she gave Danny a thumbs up sign.

"Rosamunde," said her mother sweetly, as she rubbed the bump on her head, "don't push your luck."

Chapter Nineteen

I can't believe it. I still can't believe he did that to me." Rosie was talking to herself as she packed up a box full of selected items from the basement of the magic shop.

It was nearly two weeks since they'd returned from California to Vermont. Although it was a Saturday and the shop was continuing to do bang-up business, Lydia decided to take a break and close it for the day.

Rosie sighed as she took down an unidentifiable statue that Lydia had marked Sold, dusted it, and put it in the carton. Lydia had decided it was time to get rid of a few of the more "unstable things," as she called them: a mirror that granted wishes; a cloak that turned the wearer into the opposite sex; a couple of lamps with a couple of real genies; and several other odds and ends of unknown use. Through special channels she had access to, she was able to find a serious and responsible buyer for them. The gentleman in question, a shaman who specialized in helping farmers grow good crops, promised to take good care of them and make sure they were never used incorrectly. He would be arriving shortly to pick up his purchases.

"Are you still harping on that Johnny Haines?" Lydia asked, coming down the stairs with the day's mail in her hands.

Rosie pouted. "I can't help it. How would you feel if you went over to your boyfriend's house to apologize for standing him up and found him with another girl? And then, on top of that, you discovered—through the helpful and nosy Choogie Marshak—that the real reason he was dating you in the first place was to get you to do his English paper?"

Lydia smiled sympathetically. "I guess I wouldn't feel very good. . . . But I'd tell myself he's not the only monkey in the barrel and forget him."

Rosie wasn't listening. "I'm going to *make* him like me. I know how to mix up a real love potion now. And then I'll cast that hands-off spell I never got around to using, and—"

"Rosie!" Lydia rapped out.

Rosie stopped gabbling and looked at her.

"Is that the way you want to have him? Now that you've found out what he's really like?" her mother asked.

Rosie screwed up her mouth but didn't reply.

Sorting through the mail, Lydia pulled out an envelope and handed it to her daughter. "Here's something that should cheer you up a little."

Rosie looked at the letter. It was addressed to her. She opened it and extracted a piece of stationery with pictures of baseballs all over it. "It's from Danny Pauling," she said.

"Read it aloud," said Lydia.

"Dear Rosie," she began, "I hope you and your mother made it back to Vermont okay. It's a long trip.

"Things are okay here. Dad rented an apartment about a mile away. We see him all the time. He and Mom still argue a lot, but not in the same way. It's kind of more friendly. Laura (she says hi) and I still don't know if they're going to get back together. But Mom's talking about taking us on a trip to Vermont next month when Dad goes back. We both want to visit you and your shop, if that's okay. It sounded neat when you described it at dinner.

"I had to do a composition in English yesterday. It was on the Most Unforgettable Character I Ever Met. I thought about writing about you know who, but it was supposed to be true, and I knew nobody would believe me. I wrote about my uncle Harry instead. He runs a tattoo parlor in New Jersey. He's got a lot of tattoos on himself. The best one is a gigantic hot dog on his bicep. Underneath it, it says, All Beef. They call him the black sheep of the family.

"Well, I've got to go. Say hello to your mother. Write back. And thanks. I mean it. Your friend, Danny Pauling."

When Rosie finished reading, she was smiling. "All Beef," she giggled.

Lydia laughed, too. "Told you it would cheer you up," she said.

Then the doorbell rang. "That must be Mr. LaSalle to

pick up this stuff. I'll finish packing if you let him in."

"Okay," said Rosie. She trotted up the stairs and opened the front door.

Standing on the porch was a slightly plump, likable-looking man with thick brown curls and apple-round cheeks, and next to him, an even more agreeable-looking boy, a year or so older than Rosie, with dark skin and light blue-green eyes.

"Hello. I'm Tony LaSalle and this is my son, Armand," the man said. "We're here to pick up the artifacts."

"Yes. Come on in," Rosie told them.

All the way downstairs, she couldn't help shooting glances at the boy.

"My friends call me Army," he said to her, while his father chatted with Lydia.

"Army. That's cute," said Rosie, blushing.

"Your mother's a witch, huh?"

"Yeah. So's your dad?"

"Uh-huh."

"Are you . . . ," they both began, and laughed.

"You first," Army said.

"No, you."

"Oh. Okay. Are you, uh, learning the Craft?"

"Yes. I am."

"Me, too. Are you any good at it?"

"Not too bad," Rosie replied. "How about you?"

"I'm not too bad, either." He grinned.

"Armand, you carry this, okay?" his father interrupted them. "My back," he explained to Lydia. "It's acting up again. I'll have to get my wife to make up some more of her liniment."

"Oh? What's in it?" Lydia asked.

"I don't know. But you can call and ask her. She'd be happy to tell you," said Tony LaSalle.

Army hefted the heavy box. "We don't live that far from here," he told Rosie.

"Really?" she said.

"Yeah, really. Maybe we can see each other again some time, help each other with our, you know, homework."

"Yeah. Maybe," said Rosie, with definite enthusiasm.

She and Lydia escorted Army and Tony out to their car. Rosie watched until it was all the way out of sight.

As she and her mother, shivering a bit in the frosty January air, walked back into the house, Lydia asked wryly, "Still want to make a love potion for Johnny Haines?"

Rosie paused a beat. "Not for Johnny Haines," she said, with a small backward glance.

Lydia chuckled. Although she tried not to, Rosie couldn't help joining in.

Then Lydia put her hand in the deep pocket of her pants to pull out a hanky. Instead, she found the empty brown bag from the basement that she'd decided at the last moment not to put in Tony LaSalle's box. "Ah, yes," she said, offering it to Rosie. "Lunch?"

"Sure," Rosie replied. "Why not?" And she carefully reached inside.